Answers In Time

Loves In Time, Volume 7

Jewel Adams

Published by Jewel Adams, 2022.

This is a work of fiction. Similarities to real people, places, or events are entirely coincidental.

ANSWERS IN TIME

First edition. June 13, 2022.

Copyright © 2022 Jewel Adams.

ISBN: 979-8201685140

Written by Jewel Adams.

Table of Contents

ANSWERS IN TIME
PROLOGUE

This Is the
EPILOGUE of Gamble in Time
Less spoiler sections, enjoy!

Sally held her hand up to shade her eyes as the helicopter lifted off the pavement then slid sideways over the treetops. For a second she watched the air batter the pines.

"I'm sorry Miss Mercy, there isn't anything more we can do. Maybe in the spring..."

The sheriff didn't finish the sentence and looked away from her. Sally already heard how everyone thought Angie's body might appear once the snow melted. Oh yeah, some unsuspecting hiker might stumble upon her decaying corpse. "No! She is not out there!"

"Miss..."

Pushing past the man, Sally didn't want to hear the sheriff's excuses, and she certainly refused to listen to his fake sympathy.

Sally managed to reach her car and start it. Locking all the doors she swung out of the parking lot and drove off down the road. She managed to drive a mile or more and escape the crowds before having to pull off the road because the sobs overtook her. Sally didn't fight them this time. She needed the release. More than once she lashed out and hit the steering wheel in anger. "Where are you? I know you aren't out there, not like they think! Damn it Angie, I can still feel you!"

She relived every hour of the search for Angie. It was some time before Sally regained her composure. Today had been the worst. Everyone had given up looking for her friend. There wouldn't be any more search parties.

Taking a deep breath Sally silently admitted that they would never find Angie.

She remembered seeing Joe Wind standing off by the trees, alone and away from the crowd. He watched her, too.

That man was a strange one and her rational mind said he could have killed her best friend. But something told her he wasn't the killing type, no matter how outlandish his story to the sheriff had been. "Walked into the trees and disappeared...yeah, okay, Angie is now some kind of magician!"

But even as she tried to seek sarcasm her hand closed over Angie's letter on the seat beside her. "Damn it Angie, why should I believe you? He could have forced you to write this!"

Closing her eyes Sally didn't need to open the letter again. She knew it by heart. Her head went back against the seat as the memory of that awful day replayed itself like some kind of horrid nightmare. One a person could never get out of their head...

"Call the police!"

Sally stepped in between the stranger and Aunt Belle, "Let him finish, Aunt Belle. Just calm down and listen to what the man has to say."

The woman glared at Sally as if she were as guilty as the silent man behind them. Oh yes, Madame La Cross had already screamed her verdict of guilt out for all to hear.

With one last humph of anger, Aunt Belle moved away to stand staring out of the window. Sally felt tension crimp her neck. She forced herself to turn and face Joe Wind. "Alright, you have the ten minutes you asked for. Please explain to us why we shouldn't call the police?"

"They won't find your friend, no one can."

The honest light of sympathy in the man's eyes wasn't something Sally could accept. "Where is Angie, Mr. Wind?"

For a second she didn't think he would answer. Aunt Belle must have felt the importance of the words he finally started speaking, for she slowly turned to watch him answer.

"She is no longer in this world."

"I never heard such rubbish!"

"Aunt Belle, please let him finish!" Sally didn't like having to act as a mediator for this man, but she felt whatever he said would be important...even if she might use it to hang him as Angie's murderer! The way he stared at her, she wondered if he read her unkind thoughts. But then what did he expect showing up here like this. And him being the person claiming to know what happened to her friend!

He pulled his attention away and looked at Aunt Belle, "Your niece is not here anymore. She is gone from the world we know, but she is not dead."

Sally had to give the woman credit, she didn't even flinch before him and Sally knew how painful those words were to them both.

"You can't expect me to accept this? What proof do you have?"

They both watched as he pulled an envelope from his coat pocket, "Her own words may explain this better."

For a few moments no one moved until Sally realized Aunt Belle had stepped back and away from the man, as if the letter were a weapon.

Sally held out her hand, "I'll take it."

He gave her a slight nod and placed it in her palm. Sally would recognize Angie's writing anywhere. She looked at Aunt Belle, "It's not opened, she addressed it to me."

Aunt Belle just stared at her, Sally didn't think the woman would ever forgive her for letting Angie leave that day over two weeks ago. The army of searching law officers and private detectives hadn't turned up any news of her whereabouts. Joe Wind was the first person to claim information about her.

Sally pried open the seal as if it would fall apart in her hands. She had to take a deep breath just to still the shaking in her fingers in order to read the letter.

"Dear Sally and Aunt Belle,

The fact that you are reading this means I am no longer around. Believe me when I say this is what I want. To try explaining all that has happened to me would be impossible and unbelievable. I will attempt to ease your minds about my welfare.

To start, I didn't just fall and hit my head on that boat. What happened to me was unbelievable even for me at first, but so very real. Somehow I managed to go back in time, to 1875. I married a man named James McFarlain. You may find him in the history books someplace or his brother Michael. Though it isn't important.

What is, is that I came back to our time when I woke up in the hospital. I know this is hard to accept, especially for you, Aunt Belle, but I desperately needed to get back to the past. You see I was there much longer than a day, months actually....

Please call off the search for me, Aunt Belle. I know you probably have everyone searching for me, it won't do any good and only hurt you more. Please don't do it. I love you, and I am sorry you have to be hurt like this. Telling either of you wasn't possible, you would have locked me up.

I am fine, honest and I'm with the man I love. Believe this and be happy for me, I must return to him...for our baby's sake.

ANGIE

PS. Joe Wind is being kind enough to help me.... He doesn't know why I need him to guide me in to the mountains, don't blame him. I beg you not to hurt Joe Wind, he is totally innocent.

"...I must return to him...for our baby's sake."

Baby? Oh yes, that much Doctor Blance verified, much to the shock of Aunt Belle and Sally. "A baby, damn Angie what happened to you?"

If Angie's own words could be believed, her friend's body would never be found. "I need to know for sure, Angie!"

Even Joe Wind tried to help Sally and Aunt Belle accept what Angie told them. He explained how she came to him and how he knew who she really was. "A legend...well you will be one, but maybe not for the right reasons."

Sadly, Sally knew Aunt Belle wouldn't quit looking for Angie. She would hire private detectives and pay for more search parties. A couple of industrious detectives turned up historic records of a ranch called Twin Creeks that did have an owner named Michael McFarlain. They also found a record of a marriage on board the Silver Queen of James McFarlain and one Angela La Cross.

It wasn't enough to prove anything. Sally took it upon herself to search further. She didn't find anything more on the McFarlains or the Indian called Striker. There was a small piece in a newspaper about a flood that came through the Twin Creek area and destroyed a ranch. No names were mentioned so she couldn't be sure it was Michael McFarlain's ranch that washed away.

The legend Joe Wind spoke of did mention a Sioux brave named Striker. Unfortunately, it didn't give any kind of detail that Sally could research any further. "Just enough information to make me want to believe all this."

She sat up and took a deep breath before turning the key and bringing the car to life. Glancing at the map once more, Sally checked which road she needed to take. She eased the car out on to the icy road, "I really hate snow."

Chapter 1
Uncovering the Truth

"You have to take me there. I know you remember where you took her!" Sally wanted to cry. All her arguments with the old man didn't budge his resolve. "Please Mr. Wind, please take me to the last place you saw Angie."

The silence hung in the air like a great boulder, one that nearly crushed the life from Sally before the man turned to finally face her. She could see the anger he fought to tame and wondered if she made a horrible mistake following him to his place. When she saw his pickup pass her, it seemed like the right thing to do.

It was too late for regrets, if he refused to help her Sally would find someone else to take her into the woods. She realized only this man knew the exact location, "You didn't show the police the exact place...did you?"

His chin rose in defiance before answering her glaring declaration. "I told them the truth as I told you and her aunt."

"I know that, but you never told any of us the exact location."

"I am an old man..."

"Pish posh!" Aunt Belle's favorite saying flew out of Sally's mouth before she could stop it. "You are as sharp as I am."

She caught the slight lifting of his lips, one that couldn't be mistaken as anything but a smile.

"She said you would be stubborn."

"We are more like sisters than friends."

He nodded in understanding for what she didn't say. "Why must you try to find her?" He held up his hand to stop her answer. "You may not return and still not find her."

So he did know... Sally tried not to show any emotion, "I know that Mr. Wind, but I must try."

"She is where she wants to be."

"I don't doubt that either."

Time seemed to suspend itself as he thought over her words.

"In the morning we leave, I will take you to the area. I can't promise you will see anything that will help."

Sally felt the tension ease out of her neck, "I know, thank you."

They didn't speak much more after that. Sally went into her own thoughts over what Mr. Wind said about *her* not returning. She wondered if maybe she should just accept what Angie wrote, but everything told Sally she needed to do this, needed to find the answer.

⁊⁓⁓⁓

"**I** hate snow!"

The man's soft laughter didn't ease Sally's chatting pout of discomfort. She thought about adding horses to her list of complaints, but figured the man heard enough of her grumbling the last two days on the trail.

Two days of riding through snow drifts that reached the top of her boots and still he pushed on. He told her at the start that it would take longer to reach the place because of the deep snow. Sally never realized what deep meant until now. Thankfully, most of it seemed to just swirl about as the horses pushed through it. Joe called it spirit snow, she didn't want to know what that might mean.

One thing Sally did realize was that Angie couldn't have survived out there alone. She said a silent prayer that this Striker did find her friend.

"A baby..."

"Her son called her back."

It was the most she'd heard from the man in two days. Sally urged the horse up to get closer. He never even looked at her, so she figured it was up to her to keep him going. "The doctor said she was pregnant."

"At first you wouldn't notice, but before we reached here her son showed his presence."

It took a moment for Sally to realize the horses stopped moving. She looked at Joe Wind and his arm came out and pointed to the stand of trees off to the left. She looked at them and then back at him, but he wasn't going to give her anything more.

For a second Sally wasn't sure if she should head for the trees or what to do next.

"She went towards them then disappeared."

Her lips didn't quiver from the cold, she bit down to stop the fear from taking hold. What could she say to this man, she could see his thoughts were back to that day. Sally looked towards the trees his gaze never left.

Without another question to herself Sally moved the horse out towards the tree stand. Joe Wind pulled his own horse up, stopping him from following her, but never said a word to halt her progress. Sally almost wished he would, but then she shut him out and concentrated on what lay ahead of her.

⟨◈⟩

It sounded like the crack of a rifle laced with thunder! Levi struggled to get the horse dancing under him back in control. "Whoa there big guy!"

Diablo finally came to an impatient stop, pawing the ground as he snorted out his displeasure over being spooked. The uneasy peace didn't last, within seconds a shrill filled the air!

Plow reining the horse in a tight circle Levi turned him around and dug in his heels, heading them in the direction of the scream. Whatever was going on the woman sounded desperate.

Hooper raced over the hill barely slowing the stallion as he tried to hear any sound that might help point him in the right direction. Thoughts of another woman filled his mind, but he quickly dismissed Angie knowing she would never come back to this place. Hell, neither did James McFarlain. Levi didn't figure that Michael's latest trip to find his brother would give any further clues to the man's disappearance.

There! Levi cautiously guided the horse to the far side of the hill. Whoever it was sounded hurt. He pulled the horse up and his boots hit the ground in the same motion. Even as he moved closer to her, there was no mistaking that the disheveled heap was a woman.

Large and gentle his hands turned her carefully over into his arm. The wild blonde hair fell over his forearm in waves of gold silk. "Beautiful..." Levi clamped his jaw down to prevent any more unwanted thoughts from escaping. His fingers brushed back the waves trying not to let the soft essence invade his sense as he looked at the dark bruises on her cheek and chin. "No doubt knocked you out." But who did this to her, he took another cautious look around them to see if anyone might be hiding, nothing, not even horse tracks.

He looked her over, but couldn't see any other noticeable injuries. The thought of moving her worried him, but leaving her lying on the thawing ground wasn't a good alternative.

With all the gentleness at his command Levi lifted the woman up into his arms and started back toward the stallion. "Be good boy, the lady is hurt, another tumble won't help her much." The way the big horse sniffed and looked the girl over made Levi wondered if the stallion understood him.

Levi received his answer when the horse pulled his head back and stood perfectly still for him to mount with the woman. He arched his brows over how slowly Diablo turned about once his feet set the stirrups. The horse automatically started working his way down the hill toward the ranch.

"Maybe I've been going about riding you all wrong Diablo, seems you have a thing for the ladies." The horse's returning snort made Levi laugh before his attention went back to the girl filling his arms. "She sure is a pretty filly."

Levi's gaze dropped to her hand, and he cussed over what he knew he looked for, he felt his relief that there wasn't any ring to be found. "So how did you come to be out here, away from any civilization?"

He tried to adjust her and make her more secure in his hold. Her moan stilled him, when she turned into his chest and her fingers closed over the edge of his vest Levi needed to swallow his own groan. "Damn lady, you wouldn't be do'n that if you knew how long it had been since I've been with any woman!"

Chapter 2
Amazing Discoveries

The crack of thunder kept vibrating through her and Sally shook her head to get rid of the gripping fear. "Angie! Where are you?"

Hooper needed to use his strength to hold the girl back into the pillow. More than once she seemed to be reliving her accident, but to have her calling out for Mrs. McFarlain gave Levi a store full of questions for her. He wished she would come to and give him the answers, but she seemed caught in a fever that wouldn't shake loose. Once she settled down again he wrung out the cloth in the basin and dabbed at the fine sheen of sweat on her face. The cutting bruise on her chin looked angry, he hoped the suave he brought up from the barn would help calm it down. A scar on that pert chin wouldn't be good.

After applying another swath of the ointment he placed the cool cloth over her forehead. She seemed calmer, but the fever still held her in its grip. "Two days, missy. I'd sure like to see those pretty eyes open." Levi pulled the chair closer to the bed and eased his tall body into the stiff cushions. "It's going to be a long night, lady. Too bad you can't tell me your name or how you know her, might make the night seem shorter."

But she wasn't answering.

Sally watched as his closed eyes twitched. Must be an interesting dream the way those full lips eased into a welcoming smile. He certainly could take a woman's breath away when he smiled like that. She decided it must be that sexy mustache that fascinated her. She never kissed a man with one, and she wondered what it would feel like. She felt her lips part over how it dipped just a bit on the left side.

Her gaze dropped to the tight grip he maintained on the chair arm, she didn't think he would smile much except in sleep. The feelings from the man were too strong to be dismissed and Sally's brow furrowed. A complex man, yes, she felt certain he would be one.

She'd been watching him for some time now, glad that there seemed to be more light coming into the room. Sally tried to push herself up in the bed, but stopped over the agonizing throb in her head that the movement brought back.

She looked to see if he heard her soft gasp over the pain...no, he stayed asleep. She wondered how long he'd been there with her. More to the point she wanted to know where here was?

The way his long legs stretched out before him told her he couldn't be very comfortable. Booted toes pointed up to the ceiling, and she smiled over how one foot hooked about the other. The spurs caught her attention; she tried to remember if anyone wore them? It hurt to think, but she did recall seeing some of the horse riders in the search party with them. Something told her he wasn't from the search party, no she wouldn't have missed him in any crowd.

When she brought her attention back to his rugged face, her gaze locked with his waiting dark eyes. They didn't look angry, but he certainly took all of her in with one careful scrutiny.

"Feel'n better?"

His voice sounded rich and thick like the high wind in the timbers Joe Wind took her through. "I think so."

She watched how the creases out from his eyes deepened, she looked to see if he was smiling, but no, the sternness she expected glared back at her.

"I'll go make you some coffee."

His tall body sort of reached up and worked itself out of the cramped position in the chair. Sally prayed he couldn't read her thoughts for she'd never seen a man look so damned, devastatingly handsome. She wanted to groan when her sight fell to his backside as he turned to leave the room. Every long stride seemed to vibrate through the solid cheeks of his butt and Sally sucked in her breath over the fire that took life deep in her sex from the vision!

"You okay?"

She jerked her gaze up to his and wanted to die over the knowing glint in his deep brown eyes. Did she groan out loud? "Sure, fine, I'm fine, really."

He didn't release her gaze for the longest time, "Fine is an understatement lady."

With that he turned and left her to gape after him. Sally let out a soft whistle, "Damn, who the hell is he?"

From the other room the answer came, "Levi, Levi Hooper."

His laughter echoed through the bedroom as Sally felt the color flooding her face.

"Nice to meet you, Levi." He didn't answer her, and she could hear the distant banging of what sounded like pots and cups.

Sally reached up to hold the side of her head when the throbbing starting again. Her fingers picked through her hair until they latched on the offensive thing and dragged it from the tangled lengths. The small twig made her groan, she must be a mess and the thought of him seeing her like this caused her toss the covers back. Getting her legs over the side of the high bed wasn't as easy, pulling the long lengths of the flannel nightgown away from her legs made Sally look at the door. She realized she didn't have anything on under the thick folds, "Oh my, Levi."

Sally spied the comb and brush by the wash basin on the dresser. Levi Hooper saw far too much of her already. To have him keep looking at the wreck she felt like, made Sally determined to make an impression on the man that captured her attention.

The effort it took for her to get off the bed nearly defeated Sally. Holding on to the bed post she used it to steady herself before stepping away from the support to reach the dresser. She silently counted each footstep, praying she would make it. Once her hands clasped the wood edge of the dresser she held on until the dizziness passed.

Sally took a tight grip on the brush and brought it up to gingerly pull it through the tangles, but each stroke made her groan until she bit her lip to hold back the tears.

The hand that closed over hers to take the brush away drew her attention to the mirror. Sally stared back at the scowling gaze behind her. He stood tall, the top of her head barely reached his shoulder. All she wanted to do was lean back into his strength. She let go of the brush he gently pulled on, her arm fell to her side. She tried to smile to ease the concern look he held her in. "There was a twig in my hair..."

He never looked away from her gaze in the mirror. "I didn't notice."

She would have laughed but the sudden dizziness made her sway and before she could take hold of the dresser he scooped her up on his arms. Sally gave up the struggle and snuggled up against the solid wall of muscle his chest afforded. She could feel him pull her closer into his embrace and Sally smiled as she closed her eyes over the spinning room. "You feel good Levi Hooper."

"Are you always so bold?"

"Hmm, Angie always said I was." She sensed the change in him before he placed her back into the bed. The covers he pulled over her were jerked in place and tuck in tight around her.

"Stay put."

If she wasn't so dizzy, she would have objected to the order that broached no argument. Why did he sound angry with her? Sally tried to remember what she said that could have upset him... "Angie..." Her friend's name rushed past her lips.

The sudden urgency in Sally made her fight to control the dizziness and focus on the room, something she knew she avoided before. As her gaze cleared she looked over at the dresser and the woman's articles that sat there as if they waited for her return. Her hand gripped the material of the nightgown and pulled it up to her nose. The tears she couldn't prevent flowed down her cheek and Sally realize now what she failed to notice before. She took a deep breath pulling in the scent she almost missed, yes, it was Angie's, familiar yet so distant.

"I think it is time we talked."

Levi's deep voice made Sally opened her eyes and brushed at the tears streaming down her cheek before taking the cup of steaming coffee he held out for her. He settled forward in the chair and sipped his own cup as she managed to take a couple of tastes of the strong brew.

Their gazes locked over the cup, she realized he must be a very patient man. Sally handed him the cup, afraid to move and bring on the dizziness again. He never looked away from her as he set both cups down on the floor.

"I think you best tell me how you know Mrs. McFarlain?"

He must have seen the questioning in her over the name. Sally realized she wasn't used to having her friend called Mrs. anything. "Angie?"

"Yes, Angie, how do you know her?"

Sally thought she could ask him the same questions, but decided she wouldn't get any answers without her own. "We are best friends. I came to find her."

"You are too late."

Over his announcement she tried to rise, but the hand on her chest prevented it. "You stay still, I want answers and having you pass out again won't get them spoke."

He waited for her to acknowledge his declaration. "Fine, I won't move, but what do you mean I'm too late."

He eased back studying her before answering, "She left with Striker, the Indian."

Sally felt the tension leave her, "Then he found her, thank God."

"Not sure what you are get'n at, Miss?"

It took her a moment to figure out that he wanted her name, "Sally, Sally Mercy."

"Sally Mercy, what do you mean *he* found her'?"

"Striker, he must have found Angie when she came back..." Sally's voice trailed off as the realization hit her. "Oh my God, back, she came back here...I'm here...am I?"

Levi watched the color drain from the lady's face as her big blue eyes grew larger over each word she spoke. He wasn't sure what she meant or if she even knew she was speaking out to him, but he understood when a woman was about to become hysterical, and she was damn close. "Sally, look at me!"

Those gorgeous blue eyes flew up at him almost pleading in the way they searched his for answers. "Sally Mercy, your friend isn't here." He hoped stating the obvious would bring the girl back to him, she seemed as if she slipped away from him at that moment, and he feared what that could do to both of them. He remembered how devastated McFarlain had been when Angie appeared to have left him, her body was here but if you looked, Levi kept thinking how she wasn't there anymore, he couldn't stand it if that happened to this beautiful woman.

"You said she came back, Sally. When did she come back?" He could see her trying to focus on his words and ground his teeth down not to reach out and pull her into his arms.

He tried to keep his voice gentle. "Tell me Sally, what did you mean?"

"She came back to be with Striker, for the baby. She said she had to come back for their baby." Sally looked over at her jeans wondering if Angie's note was still in them, before she could say anything Levi got up and went over to her clothes and started rummaging through her pockets until he pulled out Angie's letter.

The look on his face as he started reading prevented Sally from saying anything more. The destruction that flashed through those soft, coffee colored eyes said it all. Did this man love Angie too? Sally knew how attractive men were concerning her friend, and never had Sally been jealous of Angie, but at that moment she felt the fire in her gut flare because of this man. This one man could have come between their friendship, it was a hard fact for Sally to admit to herself.

When he finished reading the letter, he folded it up and placed it back in her pocket before turning to face her.

"She came back?"

His question sounded hollow as if he were missing something and needed her to tell him, "She did as far as I know. I thought you said she was gone, that Striker...?"

"Striker came and took her from here." Levi wondered if he should tell this woman, this friend of Angie McFarlain's that Angie was gone long before the Indian she loved came for her. The letter's words burned in his head, she spoke of traveling back in time. Levi remembered the woman that had a spirit like no other and his gaze flew back to the lady now lying in her bed.

"...I'm not sure about that Levi."

"Where are you from Sally Mercy? What time did you come from?" His questions came out harsher than he would have liked, but he wouldn't take them back. He wanted answers that only she could give him. Michael was out looking for his brother, who went searching for this woman's friend. If Levi could believe what was happening he figured only Sally Mercy could give him the answers. "What was the year when you left Sally Mercy?"

Her mouth opened to answer and snapped shut. Sally suddenly feared the answer, and the look on the man's face that waited for her to speak it.

She tried to shake her head in denial and earned a groan of pain for her efforts. "Don't Levi."

"You know don't you, Sally. That letter said she traveled back in time, those are her own words to you!"

"Yes, damn it! Angie wrote it. I came here to find her, to prove to myself that she was alright!"

"What date Sally? Tell me the date!"

Her lips quivered, but she forced the words out and seeing the shock on the man's face gave her own answer. "...so, I'm not in that time anymore, am I Levi?"

His head shook, "No, no you're not Sally Mercy and I don't know what to believe at this point."

Before she could ask him anything more he left the room, for her to stare after him. Sally spoke out to the vacant room through quivering lips, "Todo, we aren't in Kansas anymore...are we?"

Chapter 3
Unsettling Developments

The knocking on the bedroom door failed to pull her attention away from the scene outside the window. When she didn't answer she heard the door slowly open and sensed the man that stood behind her. Sally closed her eyes for a second as she took in the virile scent of Levi Hooper wondering how he could invade her so thoroughly and so fast.

"You shouldn't be up."

His husky voice sent a tremor racing through her, and she wished she could gentle the effect he wielded. "I'm fine."

The fact she kept her back to him made Levi want to take hold of her shoulders and spin her about to face him. He couldn't tell how upset she was without seeing those vivid blue eyes of hers. His gaze ran over the dress she wore. Taking her pants and shirt away as she slept, cost him her good nature, but having her come out of that room and run into any of the Twin Creek hands in those pants wouldn't do, no sir. Talk of her presence raced through all the men. Levi cleaned his guns this morning and prayed he wouldn't need to test his speed with them any time soon.

"Breakfast is on the table Sally."

His breath caught in his throat as he watched her slowly turn to face him. The bruise on her chin looked better, it would heal without scarring. But he didn't think her temper would cool anytime soon.

"Where are my clothes, Mr. Hooper?"

"In a safe place," He supposed he could explain about the men, but he remembered how Angie insisted on wearing her pants, and he didn't think Sally Mercy would listen any more than her friend. Hooper wondered if all the women of the future were this stubborn and independent.

"You could have asked me first."

His chin came up against the accusing tone she used, "Could have, didn't feel like a fight and still don't. Your choice, Sally."

The way she walked past him made him wonder if he hadn't been too hard on McFarlain for his treatment of Angie. He caught how her hand reached out and used the furniture to keep herself steady. Proud too, two women so much alike, but if truth be told he liked Sally Mercy in a different way than Angie McFarlain. Oh yeah, Levi wanted Sally Mercy in his bed and under him in the most claiming way a man could desire a woman!

He didn't bother to hold her chair, deciding she might scratch his eyes out if he got too close. He never saw a woman so angry, he suspected he'd soon get the full brunt of it.

They ate in silence, he couldn't say she ate much, but Levi kept his thoughts to himself. When she let the fork drop into the plate, Levi had a feeling breakfast just ended.

"Where is my letter from Angie?"

Levi reached into his shirt pocket and pulled it out, placing it beside her hand. He wondered if she realized how damaging that letter might be to her. "It should be destroyed." He would have to make her understand if she didn't listen.

Sally's fingers closed over the folded paper and pulled it into her lap. She refused to get emotional in front of him again, but it proved hard. "Am I really in 1875 Levi?"

He put his fork down and sat back in the chair before answering her, "Actually, it is 1877, March 17th." He waited for those blonde lashes to raise, the blue in her eyes shined in unshed tears.

"Oh my, but how?"

"Sally..."

"Forget it, it isn't important. What's a year or two when...?"

She couldn't say it any more than he could, and he wanted to dispute the whole possibility of time travel, but he realized last night that she wouldn't have known who would find her, and she certainly didn't plan on getting hurt. "How did you hurt yourself Sally?"

Her hand rose to her chin, "I'm not sure, I rode toward the trees that Joe Wind pointed to, the ones that Angie rode into to get back to Striker, I don't remember too much after that, just the loud noise and this pounding headache that won't stop."

He watched as her delicate fingers rubbed her temple as if she could make it disappear. Levi couldn't remember ever wanting to hold a woman to comfort her, but then he'd never met Sally Mercy. "You should lie down a while."

"No! What I should do is leave. Go back where I came from and I want you to take me back to the place you found me...please." She looked at him then and Sally knew she silently pleaded with him to do this for her. "Levi..."

"I'll get the horses."

Before she could reach out to touch his arm he pushed away from the table, but he stopped at the door and turned to look back at her. Sally braced herself, for what he felt he needed to say to her.

"Sally, if you can go back it would be best to know right now." She couldn't pull away from the fierce light in his eyes, "But if you can't go...back there, well then you and I, well we are going to talk."

With that Levi Hooper slammed the kitchen door. The tears fell down Sally's cheek, and she realized she hoped that she couldn't go back, not if it meant she would leave this man. Sally looked at Angie's letter and wondered how her friend ever coped with finding herself back here. Did Angie fall in love with James McFarlain as fast as she believed she just did over Levi Hooper?

Sally couldn't remember ever feeling like this for any man in her time. *My time? Am I really back in 1877?*

She refused to look around the house, just like she didn't want to see the things in Angie's bedroom, in the drawers and wardrobe. The pictures and writings that only Angie could have done, oh yes, she found those in the top of the wardrobe. Angie's drawing were the final proof that Sally truly did come back in time. She stared at the dress she wore and knew it was as real as the wood burning stove across from the table.

She crushed the letter in her hand. He was right, if anyone else saw this they would lock her up, forever. Angie must have made an impression on Levi Hooper for him to believe what he read.

She pushed back from the table and walked over to the stove. The iron handle stuck into the round plate looked hot so Sally picked up folds of her dress to hold it. The weight of the lid surprised her, Sally placed Angie's letter between her teeth in order to have the use of both hands. Once the lid was off, and she could see the coals, Sally took hold of the letter and slowly moved it over the fire before finally dropping it into the flames. She watched as it burned before she moved the lid back.

Turning, she came face to face with Levi, "I know that was hard for you Sally, but it needed to be done."

"Yes, I guess so."

They both heard the call from outside that the horses were there.

Levi pulled a coat from the peg by the door, "It snowed last night—you will need this."

She remembered the scene she saw this morning from the window, odd how she sensed Angie doing the same thing. "I hate snow."

"I don't think she liked it much either." He didn't try to hide his humor with her when that blue light in her eyes turned to sharp stone. The lady possessed a temper, Levi hoped he'd actually get to feel the fire she smothered as she turned away from him. Thoughts of refusing to take her to the hill rushed through him, but he managed to smother the desire.

Levi lifted her long hair out of the coat, and over the collar as he helped her get her coat on. He let the silken strands slide through his fingers and for a second he let her delicate scent fill his nostrils. God, he wanted to bury his face into her hair and pull her back against the hard-on he couldn't prevent, thankful that his coat hid the evidence of his desire. If she could return to her time, he wondered if he could let her. The horrible thought struck him that she might go back, and he'd never get to...

Sally swallowed her gasp as Levi spun her about and his lips came down to take hers in a possessive hold that she never wanted to end. Hard and fierce, he refused to gentle the kiss that drove to hold her to him, and she leaned into the solid length of his body as one of his arms came around her waist and the other held her head to his pleasure. When his tongue ran across her teeth she opened to him as if she knew him as a lover and Sally moaned in wanton longing to feel the man. His hand caught her wrist before her fingers could take hold of his manhood pressing against the heat of her sex.

Her eyes opened and looked in question to his as his lips reluctantly released hers. "No way lady, I couldn't let you leave if we go any further."

The truth he refused to hide from her drew her lips back to his, Sally's hands framed his cheeks to keep him close. Their hunger grew fierce as each devoured the other with the passion the shared kiss awoke.

The call from outside finally forced them to pull free of each other, but not before Levi drew her hard against him and ground her hips over the force of his need for her. "I swear I want a lot more from you than a good lay Sally and I'm going to show you the truth of my feelings if you stay, here, with me."

Chapter 4
Be Careful What You Wish For...

The cold air bit at her exposed cheeks. Sally wondered how people lived in such harsh climates and decided she was definitely a southern belle in this snow covered land.

She chanced another look at Levi, her tongue moved over her lips trying to recapture the taste of this marvelous man. That she wanted him to take her right there in that kitchen was obvious to both of them. The remembered feel of his commanding manhood pressed up against her aroused sex nearly made her moan out with the hunger he exposed. She dated many different types of men since college, but none could come close to the arousal Levi Hooper called from her. Sally figured she wouldn't be a virgin if they had, no, she knew she'd never have walked away from a man like Levi.

The horse stumbled and demanded her attention as they made their way up the hill above the ranch. Sally turned in the saddle and looked back at the small house and barn buildings. From here it didn't look as large, though when they were in the yard she knew her surprise over the number of men milling about.

A soft smile came back to her as she recalled how possessive Levi became in their midst. The way his hands gripped her waist and lifted her into the saddle, anyone would have been a fool not to notice the unspoken decree that yelled—"hands off". The guns he wore strapped to those powerful thighs said a lot just by their presence. She wondered if he would actually use them, quickly dismissing the question knowing that he would. Sally didn't doubt that Levi might be dangerous. The truth left her a little unsettled, yet she didn't believe he could ever hurt her.

Having someone like Levi Hooper staking a claim on her honestly didn't upset her as much as it would have back home. Was it the fear of being here, the fact she found herself in the time Angie came to that drove her into this man's arms? Sally still found it hard to understand how she managed to come here. The thought of going home sounded appealing, but then Levi Hooper wouldn't be in her time. A shiver passed through her over the truth of her strong feelings for this stranger.

If she did stay here how bad could it be? Angie certainly wanted to come back—for love. Love? Was that what Levi offered her a glimpse of in the kitchen? The possibility made her fidget in the saddle. She never looked for love in a man before, did she have to travel back in time to discover that elusive ecstasy?

If Angie were here. Would she be able to find Angie? Sally wondered if Levi would help her find her friend.

All the questions bombarding Sally ended the moment that Levi stopped the horses. She didn't pull away from the intense scrutiny he held her in, wishing he would act on the desire he let her see.

"This is the place Sally. I didn't see anything or anyone but you up here."

Dragging her gaze away from him proved more difficult than she wanted to admit as she looked around them. Nothing appeared familiar to her. She remembered how Joe Wind stayed back, not moving towards the trees, had he known she would go through that invisible barrier?

How could she admit to either of them that she didn't really want to find that door in time?

Sally took a deep breath and urged the horse forward.

Levi pulled his hand back from taking hold of her horse's reins. Of course she must return if she could, but heaven help them both because Levi prayed the door would close forever to Sally Mercy!

As if she heard his deepest desire she looked back at him, a look of pure fear on her face that made him dig his heels into the stallion. "What is it Sally?"

"I'm not sure, I can't move. I feel as if something has hold of me and I'm scared! Levi I don't want to go back!"

Hearing the words she spoke was all he needed. Levi made the stallion side step against her unmoving horse, and he reached over and yanked Sally out of the saddle. He felt the invisible hold trying to pull her back, out of his arm, but Levi called on every ounce of power in his possession to hold on to the woman suddenly a part of his heart.

The stallion reared and spun about as if he too could feel the force trying to get a hold of them. It seemed as if ages passed before the big horse broke free and bucked away from the power shimmering behind them. Levi held Sally to him and her arms circled his neck, holding on as if her life depended on it and Levi had a feeling it did. They raced away from her screaming horse, and Sally's scream of pure terror filled his soul as they escaped as her horse disappeared.

"No, no, I don't want to leave you, I don't want to leave you..."

Her vow kept echoing in his ears until she suddenly went silent and limp in his hold. Levi felt the fear for her seize him. He leaned down and placed his ear against her chest, thankfully hearing the rapid beat of her heart. He couldn't blame her for fainting, he wondered if she meant what she said. He sure as hell knew how he felt about her. Levi's only remaining fear rested in Sally and if he could keep holding her—in his time!

Hooper pulled the stallion up and as the horse danced around in a circle he looked back up the hill and noticed how storm clouds seemed to be gathering around the top. Memories of the night that Angie disappeared, yet remained, caused him to hold Sally tighter. Levi prayed she wouldn't get hurt, he needed to get her back to the house.

He refused to look back, never wanting to see what was happening behind them.

By the time he reached the yard the men were running around to secure the livestock and lock down the buildings against the storm now upon them. Levi tried not to expose the fear gripping him that this power might still be able to reach her, take her from him.

He called one of the men over to take the stallion as he jumped clear of the spooking horse with Sally locked in his arms. Hooper kicked the kitchen door open and headed toward the bedroom, but stopped short of going into Angie's room. No, he couldn't take her to that room, not to the same one that the power once found Angie McFarlain in.

Hooper turned and headed up the stairs to his room. Once inside he gently laid her on the bed. His fingers shook over the memory of how beautiful Sally's body truly looked as he worked off her coat. He almost turned to go and get her nightgown, but stopped himself not wanting to chance fate and pulled a nightshirt from his drawer.

"Are we tempting the fates Sally?"

His movement stilled as he watched her eyelids flutter and try to open. Levi knelt down beside the bed and took her shaking hands in his, trying to warm the cold out of them. "Come on Sally Mercy, talk to me, fight it Sally. You said you wanted to stay with me...proved it!"

"Don't yell at me Levi..."

He dropped his forehead onto their clasped hands and smiled. "I'm sorry sweetheart, you just keep telling me when I cross the line."

He let her work one of her hands free of his hold and when it came to rest on his cheek Hooper turned his head and kissed her palm. "God Sally, can we beat this thing? I want you in my life woman, am I crazy?"

"Not anymore than I am Levi. I don't want to go back, I want to stay with you."

Her declaration brought his hard gaze up to meet her overly bright one. "Do you mean that Sally? Mean the commitment I want from you?" All the old fear and hurt rushed in on him as he spoke his heart's desire. Would this woman crush the life from his heart as another once did? He carried those scars for a long time, and he sat before this stranger, this time traveler, declaring what he never wanted to say to any woman ever again!

The way her head titled to the side worried him until her lips eased into to a soft smile. "If you can feel what I do for you in such a short time, then yes Levi. I mean every word."

Sally swallowed hard over the way his dark study tried to plow its way inside of her. Whatever he looked for she prayed he would find the right answer. The wind outside seemed to howl in tune with this man's emotions.

"Don't move!"

There he went again, ordering her about. Sally hoped they would have time to sort out that bothersome quirk. She watched as he went to the window, and hit at the wooden sash to get it open. He stuck half his tall frame through the opening and called down to someone in the yard. She couldn't hear the exchange, but was glad when he slammed the window shut once again and the wind stopped blowing into the room.

His room? She noticed the work clothes hung on hooks on the wall and knew it must be his room. She turned her head sideways to take in the scent on the pillow, wishing it could enfold her.

He hated to disturb the beautiful picture she made on his bed, but Levi didn't want what was coming to happen in here. "Sally?" It took him two more tries before he gained her attention. The blush he received for his effort earned a grin through the tightness in his jaw. The wind roared like an angry animal around the house, pulling his attention back to the urgency he felt for them. "Come with me Sally."

That she didn't argue and placed her hand into his palm gave him some hope that things might work out. As he led her from the room Levi wondered how she'd take his next announcement. "I hope you don't mind not having a fancy wedding, Sally."

Chapter 5
Vows and I do

"Wedding? But Levi how can we have a wedding...now!"

"How can we not have one?" He kept a tight hold of her hand as they moved through the house to the kitchen. The storm sounded horrible when the kitchen door burst open!

Sally leaned back against Levi, his hands rose to hold her arms. For some reason she didn't think the man standing in the doorway was the person he expected to see. The silence hung between them and Sally suffered the stranger's intense blue eyes that took in every bit of her in Levi's hold.

From behind her he finally spoke up, "Michael, good to see you."

The man kept looking at her and Sally finally breathed once his gaze rose to Levi. "Hooper, seems like I got home just in time."

"Reverend should be here soon."

"That is what the boy told me."

Those crystal blue eyes looked at her in open curiosity.

"Sally, this is Michael McFarlain, Michael this is Angie's best friend. She came a long way to find Angie."

The man's shock became evident when he dropped his bedroll and stared open mouth at Sally. It took him a few seconds to regain his control and move towards them. Sally tried not to react to the tightening of Levi's fingers on her upper arms.

"Angie's friend? Really? This is quite a surprise," he looked up to Levi, "when did she come, how? We need to discuss this."

When she shifted nervously in front of him the man closed his weary eyes and dropped his head, before finally looking at her again. "I am very sorry Sally...?"

27

"Mercy, Sally Mercy, Michael." Her heart filled with feeling for this man, she noticed the pain in his eyes and knew it must be associated with Angie.

"Miss Mercy, I'm afraid Angie is gone. I haven't found her or my brother James in over a year."

Levi spoke up, "So, the last sighting wasn't James?"

Michael looked over Sally's head to Levi, "No, if it was James he made sure I couldn't follow or find him."

"Maybe he doesn't want to be found Michael."

"I guess you were right Hooper, I should have let it go last year like you said."

The wind howled about the house drawing all their attention to the rattling windows. Sally noticed the worried look that Michael shot Levi, and then tried to hide from her. Whatever the man wanted to say remained silent, and she sensed Levi must have stopped him from speaking about the concern she caught on his face.

Before any of them could do anything the kitchen door burst open behind them. Sally watched the disheveled man pushing the door close against the wind. His hat blew off and what hair he did have stood up on end atop his head, making him look like a mad scientist. The stovepipe hat he managed to settle back over the straw mass of hair didn't smooth out his image, and she wondered what he could possibly do on a ranch.

"Blowing in from the south, meaner than the devil's teeth."

She could hear Levi snicker behind her and it helped Sally relax a bit. Whoever the man might be he must be harmless or Levi wouldn't be so calm. She waited for introductions.

"So, who am I to up and marry this storm driven day?"

Without the slightest hesitation Levi spoke up, "The lady, Sally Mercy and I are going to marry, Reverend."

She suffered through the man's perusal, but it was Michael's skeptical look that upset her more than the weird man checking her out. She couldn't say if Michael McFarlain disliked her on the spot or found the whole situation more than he could tolerate. Sally braced herself for what she felt would come from him, her own lack of protest over the pending marriage felt rather odd, but she couldn't honestly find anything to say to stop the crazy ride she felt she took a seat on.

Never in her life did Sally think her wedding day would be like this. Yet, feeling the man's impressive body pressing into her back, remembering his kiss...oh yes she wanted to be Levi Hooper's wife. Be it some weird effect of time travel or just plain lust, Sally couldn't bring herself to stop it. Some deep instinct told her that she wouldn't be going back to her time and though the prospect felt frightening, being here with Levi felt oh so right.

Levi realized Sally was deep in her thoughts when she didn't answer the Reverend. His stomach felt as if a porcupine just released its quills into his gut. If she stopped the wedding he honestly wasn't sure what he would do, but Levi knew he wouldn't allow it, *no sir, he'd not let this woman leave him.*

"Sally, sweetheart, the Reverend needs you to answer him." Her hair smelled like a summer wind as he spoke against the side of her head hoping to gain her attention. He could feel her body come alive and Levi braced himself for whatever she might do next.

"Yes, young lady, I asked if you agreed with Mr. Hooper here. Do you want to marry this man?"

The man's eyes seemed to pop out of his head as he waited for her to answer. Sally fought to sort out her feelings, "Yes, yes Reverend I do want to marry Levi."

Before the man could answer her declaration, Michael moved between them. "I know I've been gone a while Hooper, but could you clue me in here. How long has she been here for starters?"

Sally knew her whole body shook under the glare that this man leveled against her. Feeling Levi's hands run up and down her arms told her he must have felt her reaction, he spoke before she could.

"Long enough for me to know I love her."

Her eyes closed over the words that sent her heart singing, she turned in his arms, ignoring their audience and looked up at him. "Do you really Levi? Honest?"

If he could believe the hope in her eyes Levi knew he could put his fears to rest. His large hands cupped her face between them, "Yes Sally, I mean every word. I know this is happening fast, for both of us, but if I've learned nothing else these past years, I realize you have to hold on to what comes your way and don't question the how or why of it."

Sally wanted to lose herself to the intensity of this man. How could she have such feelings for a complete stranger? But he wasn't that at all to her. Sally suspected they knew each other better than most people ever got to know one another. "Shall we get married then?"

Her smile met his descending lips with the hunger they both wanted to sate. The Reverend's cough finally drew them apart.

"Better hurry Reverend, I don't think I've ever seen a man that wanted to marry someone as bad as Hooper does Miss Mercy."

Sally returned the smile from Michael over his declaration. He still held questions, and she wondered how she would ever give the answers, she knew he wanted. Did he know about Angie and where she really came from? The answers weren't going to be easy.

Chapter 6
Hunger, Sex and...

Sweetheart? Did Hooper call this girl that? Michael tried to concentrate on the vows being spoken by his friend and the stranger becoming his wife. But as hard as he tried to accept what he heard from Hooper, he wanted to step in and call a halt to the wedding. Never, not in over ten years did he ever hear Hooper talk this much and never did this man allow anyone to call him—Levi!

Michael watched to see if he could detect any hesitation on the man's part as the Reverend told him what to repeat back to the girl. If Hooper wasn't being such a contradiction to the hard bastard Michael knew him to be, he'd say a stranger stood before him. Who would think that Hooper, of all men, could fall hard and fast for a woman? But nothing Michael saw said otherwise, and he certainly couldn't dispute the love shining from those beautiful eyes of Hooper's bride.

A summer breeze in winter? Where Angie was all dark and exotic in looks, her friend shined in a beautiful light that no man could miss. Blonde as an angel, a truly gorgeous lady, Hooper sure picked one lovely woman to fall over.

As the vows ended Michael tried to keep his smile in place though his mind kept spinning under all the questions that he wanted to ask Mrs. Levi Hooper.

The Reverend passed Michael the marriage papers to witness after Hooper and his new wife put their signatures on the document. He couldn't help but look under Sally's signature to see what she put down as her home. Just the state Louisiana stared back at him. When he looked up he met her gaze and knew she caught him, if she were upset she hid it well. The understanding smile she gave him eased the stiffness in his neck and shoulders over any condemnation he expected from her.

31

When it came time for congratulations Michael caught the instant tensing in Hooper when the Reverend hugged Sally. He decided a small peck on her forehead shouldn't get him decked on Hooper's wedding day.

As if Mother Nature sighed the wind settled to a softer blow and house stopped shaking. They all looked around at the windows that no longer rattled, Michael caught the way Levi tightened his grip about the woman's shoulders and how he smiled down into her questioning gaze upon her new husband. Michael's curiosity mounted for this woman, and he didn't bother to camouflage them from Hooper's stern glare.

Sally didn't fail to see the silent, but no less potent, exchange between Levi and Michael. She didn't want to come between friends, and neither did she want her wedding night marred with anger. She made up her mind to speak to Levi.

Levi felt this overpowering force to shelter his—wife? Yes, that is exactly what she became, and he wanted to shout to the world how lucky he felt. He could understand Michael's mounting questions, but nothing or no one would be allowed to hurt Sally. His gaze fell away from Michael over the pressure Sally gave her hold on his arm.

He prayed that smile of hers never ended. "It is all right, Sally."

She wanted to soften the determination in his gaze. "No, we both know he has questions and I'd rather answer them now." When he would have ignored her, Sally placed her hand on his cheek to hold his attention to her. "I don't want anything to ruin our wedding night, Levi." Sally didn't release her breath until his head turned, and he kissed her palm.

"Once the house settles down we will answer Michael's concerns."

She smiled up at this extraordinary man. "That is fine, Levi." She looked over at the dark scowl glaring at the two of them. "Go and tell him, Levi, he's close to exploding."

Levi leaned in and kissed away her concern. "He'd best remain a gentleman."

Sally didn't have to ask what Levi meant. In the short time she knew him, she already determined that no one took Levi Hooper lightly.

Hooper, Sally liked the feel of her new name. She kept the two men in her attention, while she accepted well wishes from the string of men that suddenly filled the house.

L evi could see the tiredness in Sally. He started to move to end the festivities, but Michael's raised hand stopped him from leaving her. The crowd quickly faded away under Michael's strong guidance.

Sally leaned back into the comfort Levi offered. For a second she closed her eyes against the draining tiredness. Time travel certainly proved to be a rough mode of transportation. For a second Sally shivered over the force she remembered that brought her here.

"Are you alright, Sally?"

"Hmm, tired is all, I guess it takes a while to get over the effects."

Levi held her closer knowing what she spoke about; even now he never doubted how she came to be in his life. "Do you regret..."

She moved faster than he expected as her hand covered his mouth.

"Don't say it, Levi. We can't ever speak of it." She knew the fright shined in her gaze by the concerned scowl he looked down at her with. The storm still raged outside, the force of it might have gentled, but Sally never wanted to wake that beast again. She slowly lowered her hand away from his lips.

He pulled her to his chest, his hand moved down the length of her silken hair trying to calm her down. "It will be alright, Sally, it will be fine."

Michael should tell them he was back, but watching them, the love he witnessed seemed to draw him in. When Levi finally looked up at him, the spell broke and Michael shook himself out of the trance.

"Everyone is gone."

"Thank you, it has been a long day for Sally."

Michael didn't doubt Hooper's statement; he could see for himself how tired she became. "Maybe we should wait and talk tomorrow."

It was Sally that stepped forward. She smiled at Michael, "No, you need the answers though I doubt I'll give you much more than you know."

Michael noticed her hand slip into Hooper's as he moved to stand beside the chair she sat down in. The man met his questioning gaze and nodded.

"All right, then how did you get here?" Michael didn't miss the tightening of Hooper's hand on hers.

Sally looked up at Levi and smiled to ease his worry before answering his friend's question. "I can only remember part of the journey..." She could see his brow raise in question. "My guide left me up in the mountains and I remember a loud noise."

Michael leaned forward when she stopped. "What else?"

Her gaze never left his. "That's it, next thing I remember is Levi."

Hooper waited for his friend's incredulous glare to flash on him. "I heard thunder and a scream, and found her up on the hill, unconscious and alone, with a hell of a knock on her head and chin."

Sally's hand unconsciously went to the tender bruise and bump at the back of her head. "I'm just glad Levi found me and that I ended up here."

"I'm sorry, but how exactly did that happen?" Michael couldn't sit still any longer and began pacing in front of them.

"I don't have an answer for that, Michael. I just know that this is where I wanted to be, to find Angie."

"She's been gone for some time now."

"That is what I understand...it took a while to get here."

"I don't know where she is."

Sally wanted to ease this man's turmoil, "I know she is with Striker."

He spun on her over that statement. Sally felt Levi tense, her other hand stopped him from moving against Michael. "She wrote me a letter, it is what brought me here."

"Where is it?"

"The letter?" She knew exactly what he meant.

"Yes."

"I don't have it anymore. I lost all my possessions." She spoke the truth, maybe not the way he heard it, but the results were what she wanted.

"All right, I have just looked for answers for so long." Michael studied the woman and found nothing that said she spoke anything but the truth. "Is there anything else her letter told you?"

He watched her worried look at Hooper. "Please Sally."

Her attention went back to the man, knowing what her announcement might do to him. "It isn't something you probably want to hear, Michael."

"After all that has happened I think I'd rather know."

She studied him a minute, "Angela was pregnant with Striker's child."

The blow of her words sent Michael staggering back into the chair that met his legs.

Hooper never let go of Sally's hand now tightening in his grip. He knew she handled the situation better than he would have, and Michael did deserve to know the truth about the child and Striker. "Michael, Angie wanted to be with Striker."

Sally spoke up when the man refused to acknowledge Levi's truthful statement. "It is the truth, Michael. She said she needed to be with him for their child."

When his gaze rose she met the dark intensity that wanted to hit someone. "He took her!"

She couldn't help but look at Levi for help.

He stepped forward releasing her hand. "And she loved him, I saw it when James brought her back." Michael's temper didn't stop the truth Hooper always wanted to speak. "She begged me not to kill Striker! Hell, James knew it, Michael. He just refused to believe it."

"Then why did he go after her?"

"Pride, anger, only James can answer that one and he's obviously decided not to do that."

Sally nearly gasped when the man's attention swung back to her. She'd never seen such fury in one person and it hurt to know that Angie caused all this pain. "I'm sorry, Michael."

"Then why are you here if you knew this?"

"Angie is more like my sister and I need to know that she is happy and safe. I have to know." She couldn't help but look at Hooper. The hard gaze he maintained on Michael didn't ease Sally's emotions. "I need to find her..."

"You and the world need that..."

Michael's harsh retort made Hooper move between his friend and his wife. She was that to him.

Michael didn't miss the man's immediate stance against him and held up his hand in defeat. "I'm sorry, Sally." He took a long, hard breath and sat back hard in the chair, his hands raked through his hair for control. "I've been looking for a long time and never found a trace of her or my brother."

Sally fought back the tears of sorrow she felt for this man and her friend. "I, too, am sorry, Michael, I wish I came with answers, but only questions followed me here."

Their gaze met and he finally nodded in understanding.

It took all of Michael's strength to pull back and not badger the girl with his questions, ones he felt she couldn't or would never answer. "Thank you for talking with me, I realize it must be difficult for you not to know what happened to her."

She looked up at Levi, and he could feel the loss they all felt. "Michael, I think Sally is tired, she's still getting over the fall..."

"Yes, of course, you two go on."

They both watched the man move one way than the other, before grabbing his bedroll and heading out the kitchen door.

"Michael?" Hooper's voice stopped him before he disappeared.

The man turned and laughed softly at his friend. "Later, congratulations on your wedding."

With that he shut the door. They could hear his laughter fading on the wind.

"Levi?"

"He'll be back, later." He smiled over the awareness slowly filling her eyes. "Come on, Mrs. Hooper."

Sally placed her hand in his as he pulled her up out of the chair. She caught the twinkle in his eyes as he moved towards the stairs. "I like the sound of that, Mr. Hooper."

Her laughter filled the air as he lifted her in his arms and took the steps two at a time to reach the bedroom. He entered the room and turned in slow circles with her in the middle of the room. "You are my wife, Sally Mercy Hooper. I don't recall ever feeling happier than I do over that fact."

Sally's finger raised and traced the proud line of his brow, down his cheek to the lips she wanted to taste once again. "I never expected to find love when I rode through that..." She couldn't make herself say the words that held too much fear for her. She took a deep breath and smiled to ease his concern. The thought that Angie must have felt like this about Striker, helped Sally understand her friend's actions. "I will stay, I know this is right and where I belong, with you, Levi."

Chapter 7
Honey Ol' Moon

Levi couldn't stop staring in wonder at the woman now a part of his life. He didn't care how she came to be here only that she stayed with him. "I've never felt like this Sally." He loved the way her emotions glowed in her eyes. The deep blue burned in warmth into his own wondrous amazement.

The howling wind seemed to cut through the trance that held them. He caught the fear lingering inside her. "It will be all right, Sally."

"Do you really think it will stop?" She tried not to be afraid, didn't want it to steal away the fire she felt consuming them, but... "Will I st..."

This time it was his fingers that silenced her words. "It will and you must, I don't think I would survive loosing you, Sally."

The honesty in his declaration allowed a tear to fall. She leaned into this hand as his knuckle brushed it way. "I won't ever leave you, I promise Levi."

"I believe you." His lips captured the velvet perfection in his hold. Levi felt the flames of passion she brought back in his life rise with a fierce intensity. The way her small hands moved over his chest drew a low groan of desire from somewhere deep inside him. "Damn, you are one powerful woman, Sally Hooper."

Levi picked up the woman he couldn't and never wanted to let go, and gently lowered her down on his bed. That shy smile she seemed to hold for him came unbidden and Levi thought he could reach out and capture its essence. He watched in wonder as she slowly eased each tiny button of her bodice through the holes. Each release drew in his breath as the heat flared over him. She looked like an angel when she pulled the combs from her hair and let the wild curls float about her in wanton abandon. He recalled how relieved he felt that she had it up and no one else could see the rich, lush waves.

When she started to push the sleeves down her arms Levi reached out and covered her hands. "Let me."

Sally couldn't breathe against the rush of feelings the touch of his fingers could create. She closed her eyes over the sensation as his hands moved down the length of her arms freeing her of the material. Her head fell back as he pulled the dress away from under her hips and the night air kissed her exposed skin.

"Pure beauty—my wife."

In wanton abandon she slowly looked at the man before her. "Oh husband, I want to see—all of you."

Levi didn't move when her delicate fingers took hold of his belt buckle and pulled the leather through the strap. In slow, glorious abandon she pulled the belt through each loop until it fell to the floor. He couldn't help but suck in his breath when the back of her fingers brushed across his abdomen as she pulled out his shirt tail and worked to release the metal buttons of his pants. With each nearly silent release he felt her move over the hardening power of his manhood.

He couldn't stop from touching her and his fingers rushed into the silken length of her hair as she bent over to push his pants down. When she could go no further than his boots, he slowly pulled her back up before him. She barely met his shoulder in her bare feet, and he realized how small she truly was. For one overwhelming moment he wondered if he might be too much for her. "Sally?"

"It will be fine, Levi. I want you to love me, show me what it feels like to be loved by you, my dear, dangerous and sexy husband." Her voice held all the husky passion flowing through her.

He couldn't help snorting over her words but quickly silenced his humor when she looked up at him in all sincerity. She felt like silk and satin under his work hardened fingers, and he couldn't get enough of her. "I want to love your body Sally the same way I feel about you."

Her head tilted to the side as if she knew he left something unsaid. "I won't break, Levi."

"But..."

"Yes, I'm a virgin..." Sally deliberately placed her hand over the power of his desire. "And you are my husband. I trust you, Levi."

Of all the things she could have said to him the honesty he heard and saw in her filled his entire being. He captured the lips she raised to meet him with and devoured the loving intensity she refused to tame. Levi realized at that moment that Sally could never lie to him, never deceive him, and he allowed himself to believe in what she willingly gave to him. His hands quickly dispersed the rest of her clothes as he worked off his boots and pants. Their laughter filled the room as both tore at each other's clothes until they were finally naked.

In awed wonder his palms cupped her peach tipped breasts marveling over their soft weight. He could feel each breath she took, each gasp as he touched her. "You are beautiful, Sally."

"I never knew a man could be so magnificent." Sally couldn't get enough of his awesome body. She'd seen many weight builders and gym fanatics, but Levi was pure power and all man. "My goodness..."

His finger came under her chin and raised her gaze back to his own. "It will be fine, Sally."

She looked at him and saw the depth of his love for her. "We really are together."

He smiled, "For all time, Mrs. Hooper."

Sally watched as he lowered his lips to take hers. In awed splendor she opened under the thrilling pressure. Wild and untamed she met him, tongue battling tongue, she moaned as he pulled her to him and ground her heat against his arousal. The touch sent her senses crazy. Sally grew bold and pressed harder, moving in deliberate slowness over the length and breadth of his manhood. Her fluid flowed hot and heavy as she coated him.

His moan drew hers. He lifted her up, and she wrapped her legs around his thighs, refusing to end the contact. It took her a moment to realize they were in the bed, but she groaned out his name as he worked the large head over her wet folds. "Oh Levi, you make me feel so hot. I want you inside."

"Patience, sweet lady, we've only just started." With that said Levi captured the succulent tip of her breast and drew hard, rolling his tongue over the areola until she raised her hips to find him. He didn't stop with one, his hand kneaded the one he left. Her cries filled the room as she buried her fingers in his hair as if to hold on. His large palm moved across the satin tightness of her stomach to cover the soft fluff of her sex. He closed his eyes over the insane sensations that touching her set loose. She pressed up into his hand and his finger dove into the soft riches, sending out her sexy purr. "You like this, Sally?"

"Don't stop, Levi, just don't stop."

She became a wild thing in his hold as he played with the swollen nub of her passion. Every stroke drew out her fluids. He could sense how close she was to climaxing and Levi slowly eased back knowing she was ready for him. He moved the tip of his erection over the length of her slick folds until she became used to his touch and moved to meet him.

Her hands captured his cheeks and brought him back to her. "I want you in me, Levi."

He smiled over her fierce statement. He kissed her lightly, "Just making sure you are ready, Sally."

"Oh Levi, I'm more than ready. I think I've waited my whole life to find you, Levi Hooper."

He pressed against the entrance of her heat, moving in slowly then pulling back, forcing himself to go slow and gentle. "I'm so glad you found me."

Sally's head fell back with the joyous laughter before she looked at him in all the seriousness she felt. "So am I, Levi, now show me how to love you."

"Gladly, Mrs. Hooper."

Hooper's knees spread her thighs as his hands took hold of her hips and moved her into position before him. He'd never seen anything so sexy as Sally at that moment. Her eyes were on fire watching him, the way she raised her hips to recapture what he held back earned his smile. "It will hurt..."

"I know it will be okay." She hoped her words were true for she never realized how large a man could be.

His lips found hers to draw her attention away from what would soon happen. All the while he kissed her his tongue moved in and out mimicking what his manhood was doing to her silken sex. All in one move he took hold of her hips and plunged pass the tight seal of her virginity. His lips smothered her deep groan. Holding himself inside her he could feel her beginning to relax. With a slowness that took all his control to maintain he began to move inside her until she started to meet him.

All gentleness became lost under the excited thrust Sally pushed up to meet him with. Levi smiled before retaking her lips and together they set a rhythm that tamed the storm.

She cried out his name as the throes of her climax overtook her. Levi held her close and plunged deep, releasing his own rush as his seed filled her womb.

As they both calmed Levi moved to her side and pulled her with him. His hand soothed down the wild shivers still running through her body, his lips kissed her brow. Levi took a deep breath and tightened his hold over the wonder in his arms. "Sweet lady, I'm so glad you found me."

⁂

The sky barely shined with the new sun peeking over the mountains, but Sally hardly noticed. No, her attention rested on one man, her husband. Her fingers played with the wild curl that fell down his forehead. She sighed over the memories of their many couplings during the night. "You are a marvel, Mr. Hooper."

She still felt like pinching herself to see if all this was real. Did she really marry him?

Under a deep breath her satisfied smile held its own life. "I'm glad I made that pact with Angie."

Hooper couldn't remain passive any longer. Her feathery touches were turning him on again, not that he minded. "What pact, Sally?"

She nuzzled his ear and laughed softly over his surprised question. "I thought you were sleeping."

He moved fast over her, his lips found that tender spot at the base of her neck that sent her crazy. He smiled over the roll of her hips against his arousal. "You are a tease, Mrs. Hooper."

She kissed his sexy lips. "Hmm, it feels so nice." She saw his brow raise and she sighed. "Oh fine, we promised each other that we would stay virgins until we married." Her finger traced the full line of his lip. "And I'm so very glad I kept that promise."

Levi pulled her finger into his mouth and sucked hard before releasing it as he ground himself against her heat. "So am I."

There were no more words for Levi found himself impatient to take her again. He wanted all of Sally and some base instinct told him he wanted her more than a man wanted a woman.

Sally could feel the difference each time they made love. This time Levi felt fierce and wild, driving her to heights she'd not touch before. She cried out his name and his arms captured her to him. She felt safe in his hold and never wanted to leave the haven he created for her.

He took her hard with a power he'd not used with her before and Sally gloried in this man. She was glad he didn't treat her as if she would break, she refused to let him right from the first. As he drove into her she could sense the claim he was staking on her. Her hands tried to sooth the force surrounding her, reassure him she was his and his alone. "I'm yours Levi, only yours. I love you."

He rose above her and stilled his wild thrusts. Sally didn't shy away from the invasion of his search, she hoped he found his answers.

Levi couldn't believe she lay there, so open, so real and honest with him. "Sally, I love you too." His lips acknowledged the depth of his words as their loving sealed his claim over the woman he held.

Chapter 8
The Wonders

"Now, hold it with both hands as I showed you."

Sally tried to concentrate on the gun, but all she could feel was the length of Levi's body pressing into her own. The way his strong fingers moved over her hand nearly made her groan.

Levi brushed his lips over her ear, "You aren't paying attention, Mrs. Hooper."

He heard her soft moan and smiled.

She took a deep breath and looked at him under the passion he stirred to life by his presence. "You make it very difficult to concentrate, Mr. Hooper."

"I promise to answer what I see in your eyes, but first the lesson."

He loved the way she tossed a pouting look at him. His gaze fell to the soft sway of her hips as she retook her stance with the gun. "Pull back easy on the trigger and be ready for the kick."

Sally bit down on her bottom lip to prepare for the gun. She eyed the target and followed his instructions. As if in slow motion the bullet left the gun, and she watched as it hit the target. "Yes!" She turned and smiled at him. "I hit it!"

His laughter came for her excitement. "Yes, you did hit it. Try it again, Sally."

She didn't miss the serious tone that entered his voice. With a great effort she focused on the target again. "I think I have the hang of it, Levi." She shot three times and hit the target each time, as he instructed her to she released the pressure on the trigger and made sure the hammer was down before lowering the gun. She felt his arm come around her and took away the gun in her hand. She wanted to lean back into his strength, feel his arms hold her in that awesome power only he possessed.

He moved closer and drew in a deep breath to capture the wild flower scent that spoke of Sally. "You did real good, Mrs. Hooper."

"I had a good teacher, Mr. Hooper." She turned and looked up at him, close but not touching, she saw the heat flooding him. "Will you teach me how to draw the gun?"

She closed her eyes as his lips pressed into her brow. "No way."

Her giggle came unbidden over his use of her favorite saying. "Levi, I should know how to do it."

"That's not something you need to know. Shooting it, straight, that's good enough."

There was no kidding in his voice and Sally wondered what upset him. That he closed himself off from her worried her even more. He moved off towards the stable, and she nearly ran to keep up with him. "Well, in that case, I'm glad I at least know how to load it and shoot it, and hit what I aim at."

"You did real good." He stopped abruptly, and turned in time to catch her before she plowed into him. "I will take you out and teach you how to use the rifle."

"Hunting, I need to know how to hunt." She looked up at him and smiled, deciding he didn't need to know that she was familiar with rifles. "Just in case." Throwing his favorite reason back at him earned his look skyward before he nodded. She rose up on tip toe and whispered in his ear, "I think I'm learning a lot, Levi, thank you." She gave him a quick peck on the cheek before he could move away.

She watched him a minute before following him to the barn. Oh yes, Mr. Hooper was a good teacher and Sally certainly needed a lot of lessons. She blushed over some of the lessons. She'd been serious that first morning after their wedding about how inadequate she truly felt here. She didn't know how to light the stove of use the oven until he showed her. Thankfully, only Michael saw her ineptness at everyday tasks. He looked at her once and just said she reminded him of Angie.

Hooper took it upon himself to educate her about life in his world, as he called it. Oh yes, Sally knew he believed her. The hours they spent talking about her world, and what would come, Levi wanted to know it all. They spoke about their future and what he felt could be done to insure they had a good one.

They spoke of so many things. Sally enjoyed their time together and still felt amazed over where she was and Levi. She did tell him that she wanted to find Angie. He was honest with her and told her that they might never find her.

She remembered..."Levi? When do we leave?"

He wasn't surprised by question and wondered when she would ask. "I spoke to Michael about it last night."

She looked up at him when he hesitated. "And, what did you decide?"

He loved the way she never let him slide by with anything. "He needs my help with the breaking and getting the horses and the cows to the buyers. But, after we get the cows to Miles City you and I will leave."

"Did you warn him about the flood?" Sally worried about the article she read and hoped she remembered the year right. If she did have the right year then next spring the valley would flood.

"I told him—your dream." He feared this part of Sally, for her well-being. Michael wasn't blind to the woman or her strange ways. *So much like Angie* is what he keeps saying. Thankfully, knowing Angie helped Michael accept Sally. "We are going to build a new house and barn up on the bluff, he's already put men to work on them."

"Thank goodness, Levi."

"He believes you, Sally."

"I know, I just hope I got it right." She didn't dare say anymore, they both knew how dangerous it might be to talk about it where someone could hear.

"Sally, Michael needs me, I can't leave for long."

"I know, but we do need to try and find her."

Hooper understood his wife's need to find her friend, "She may not want to be found."

It was a hard fact and one Sally knew she needed to face. "True."

He pulled her into his embrace and held her until the shivers running through her calmed down. "Better?"

"Always, when you hold me."

"Then I need to do it more often."

Her hand raised and touched his cheek. "All the time would be nice."

Michael smiled over the loving picture they made. "Glad to see the honeymoon is still in full swing."

Sally's soft laughter eased Levi's embarrassment over getting caught being affectionate in public. She was learning that her Levi wasn't the man these men knew. It astounded her that they couldn't see the caring, gentle and compassionate man that he truly was. Of course, she realized he could be temperamental, even a crouch and yes, dangerous. Those guns he wore weren't there for show, and she had a feeling she didn't want to see how fast he could be.

Her brow furrowed as she wondered if that is why he withdrew from her when she asked about drawing the guns. It wasn't something he would talk about—not yet.

She cleared her thoughts to listen to Michael and Levi's conversation about the horse herd.

"We will need to get them to come into the corral."

"That's not going to be easy, Diablo isn't going to let us get near him or his mares."

"What if you captured that mare, Lady, I heard you talking about the other day. If you had her he might follow." Sally blinked over the way both of them swung about and stared at her. She was ready to apologize when both men smiled at her.

"Sally, I think you are right. He would follow Lady and she won't be that hard to get." Michael could feel the relief ease off his shoulders knowing she was right. "Thank you, at least it is a better idea than anything we thought of trying."

Levi agreed and kissed her quick as they walked past her. "I'll just go up to the house..."

Their waves made her turn and head to the house. "Men. They do get into it all the way."

The house felt nice and warm after being out in the crisp air. Sally automatically checked the fire in the stove and fed it some more wood. She needed to get the stew pot from the root cellar and she glared at the door. Going down there was the one thing she didn't like doing.

She searched for a candle to take with her. The steps were rickety, she at least wanted light to see where she should put her feet. When Levi showed her the cellar she actually moaned when he told her that is where she should go if ever there were an Indian attack or other disturbance. That he was serious left no room for arguments from her. One thing Sally learned about Levi was that when his voice went deep and his stance took on that harder than stone look, there was no budging the man. He would refuse to listen to anything she might say.

In all honesty Sally knew he was right—"So far."

She blew out the match that lit the candle and opened the cellar door. "Any critters down there, you just scurry away for a while. I only need to get a few things."

Once her feet touched the dirt floor she breathed a bit easier and placed the candle on one of the higher steps to light the room.

"We need a darn cat." Sally refused to let the scurrying noise in the cellar get the better of her. "Shoo, go on and get back in your holes!"

She placed the pot and some other dishes that she needed for dinner on the steps, moving each item up as she made her way back to the top. One by one she pushed them out onto the kitchen floor, and then she blew out the candle relieved when she could shut the door. "I have watched too many scary movies."

Fixing dinner and the house, became her responsibility after that first week. "A month already, my goodness time..." Sally snapped her mouth shut refusing to say the words. She feared any reference associated with how she came to be here. She remembered how long Angie was here when it was only a night there. The difference still amazed her when she found out. "How did you survive, my friend?"

No one spoke of James, not even Michael. From what little Levi told her about what happened and how the man reacted towards Angie—she shivered over the thought of Angie having to deal with all that anger. From what little she learned from Joe Wind, Angie and Striker were a legend passed down through his tribe. Joe Wind told her of the dark haired, green eyed woman that walked the plains to return to Striker. He also told her how her baby made himself known the closer they came to the place.

"I'm glad she found him."

"Who did she find, Sally?"

"Michael, I didn't hear you come in. I'm just rambling to myself."

"About Angie?"

She couldn't help but see the darkness saying her name brought to him. "Yes, Angie, she found Striker for their child."

There she said it. She wanted to take it back over the paling in the man before her. "I'm sorry Michael, I never should have said anything."

"No, I guess I knew. She was sick and couldn't eat, I just never said it because of James."

"I know she loved him too. I don't think I would survive what she went through." Sally turned away knowing she said too much and busied herself with dinner. Michael left without saying or asking anything else.

Dinner was a quiet affair and more than once Levi looked at her in concern. She would answer his unspoken questions when they were alone, knowing he wouldn't like that she and Michael spoke of Angie again.

She pushed her food around and was glad when it was over. Doing the dishes felt like a relief at least until Levi came and picked up the towel to dry them.

"Okay, let's have it, what's going on between you and Michael?"

She couldn't look at him and forced herself to answer. Sally told him what she told Michael.

He took hold of her shoulders and turned her to face him. "Sweet lady please don't put yourself in danger like that."

"You know I didn't mean to, I was just talking to myself. It was that darn cellar, gave me the willies."

He wanted to shake her and all he could do was pull her to him and hold her. "Sally, please, you need to be careful."

"I know, Levi." He smelled good, like the wind as it blew across the valley.

Michael moved back into the shadows deciding not to bother them. Her words about Angie kept going through his head. There was something he couldn't find the answer to concerning Sally. "What does she mean, Angie found Striker? The man took her from here."

"Let it go, Michael, please." Hooper stood behind Michael and waited for his friend to turn and face him. "Just let it be."

Michael shook his head, "I wish I could."

"Don't hurt her, Michael. Don't ever cross that line."

Michael watched his lifelong friend turn and walk away. He'd seen that look in Hooper before, but never had it been directed at him. "I've been warned."

The admission made him suck in his breath. He cursed his own stupidity. Only a fool would ignore how protective Hooper became concerning of his wife. Maybe it would be better for them to leave for a while. If he didn't need Hooper's help so much he'd tell him to go now, but of course the man wouldn't. No, he'd not leave Michael in a fix.

Michael turned back to the window and told himself he needed to stop badgering Sally about Angie. He valued Hooper's friendship too much to test the man.

⁓

Sally pulled her feet up under her and covered them with her nightgown. She scolded herself for sitting up and not getting back into bed with Levi. But her head was full of worry over him tonight, and yes, Michael too.

The moonlight glowed around Levi enhancing his virile body. Her arms closed about her knees remembering what that magnificent body could do her. She wished he could fold those powerful arms about her and keep her safe all the time. Yet, that same protective desire was coming between two friends and Sally wasn't sure how to prevent what she felt would happen.

Maybe...no, she couldn't do that, couldn't stop looking for Angie, could she? Her heart felt as if it would break, for the truth rose up and said she should. If she gave up the desire to find her friend then the tension in this house would fade away. Michael and Levi could remain friends.

Sally felt the hot tears running down her cheeks and brush angrily at them. The answer she wanted to find rose up in all its glory and nothing would make it go away.

"Sally? Why are you sitting up and freezing? What's wrong?" Hooper's intense scrutiny on his wife caught the glint of tears she tried to hide. "Sally?"

"I'm fine, Levi."

Throwing back and covers he pulled his legs over the bed, "like hell you are."

He lit the lantern and slipped the glass back over the base. "You want to tell me what's upset you?"

"No."

One thing he'd figured out about his wife is that she didn't mince words, especially when she was upset over something. "How 'bout we talk about it anyways."

"Go back to bed..."

"Not happening, Sally. I have a feeling this is one of those times we need to talk things out and not let them stew."

She gave him a sharp glance before pushing off the chair and grabbing a blanket from the bed.

He watched her wrap herself up in the blanket and settle back into the chair. The fact she ignored him set a fire off deep inside that he refused to put out.

When he rose and moved towards her Sally knew what he would do. "No Levi, now just stop it!"

"Nope." He ignored her angry pout as he lifted her in his arms and then settled himself into the chair with her in his lap. She'd done such a good job of wrapping herself up to stay warm that she couldn't use her hands to fend him off. "Now, we will talk."

When she turned her face away he wanted to yank it back, but he had a feeling physical force wouldn't get him any closer to answers than her silence. "How about I start—you are trying to figure out what is wrong with Michael and me."

The way she turned about and faced him gave him a pretty good idea that he found the problem. "Might as well talk about it, Sally."

"Oh really, just spit it out?"

"Sounds about right."

"Then by all means Levi Hooper, just spit it on out there."

Her righteous glare earned his stern look.

"And that's what I thought, it is okay for me to spill my guts but let's not hear from the other side." Sally felt ready for a fight.

"I told him not hurt you."

She blinked over his softly spoken words. "Oh." She turned her head to the side and looked at him, "he didn't hurt me, Levi, honest. I never should have said anything. It is my own fault."

"Maybe, but if he doesn't back off you will get hurt and that is something I won't stand for."

"I know..." Her hand wiggled free and came up to cup that fierce jaw of his in her palm. "I love you and I'm sorry I tried to pick a fight and take my anger out on you."

His head turned and kissed her palm. "No problem." He knew she would smile over using her saying back at her. "You are forgiven, but don't hide from me, Sally. You need to talk things out with me, okay?"

Her gaze faltered before meeting his again, "You're right."

"Then let's start now. What's got you upset besides Michael?"

She wondered how he could read her so well. "I want to forget about looking for Angie."

"Sally..."

She stopped him from saying anything more, "no, I mean it, Levi. My life is not with her any longer that is a fact, no matter how much it hurts. It is with you, and for now or always Michael and this ranch are a huge part of our lives. Going off looking for a shadow would be foolish when I've so much right here. You are my world, Levi, only you, not Angie, not anymore."

His fingers rubbed away the tears she failed to stop. "And these?"

"They are for the loss I feel for a friend I'll never see again."

Levi pulled her up against him, and she folded herself around him. He stroked her hair as she cried. "I love you, Sally."

Her arm tightened about his neck.

It was a long time before her tears ended, and she fell asleep in his arms. Levi didn't bother moving them back to the bed. He sat there holding her as the sun started to rise. She wasn't the only one that made some decisions, ones he would take care of today.

⟨◈⟩

"Are you sure this is what you want to do?"

He turned and took hold of her shoulders to slow her down. "Yes, now go on back to the house."

Sally nodded as he kissed her brow and left her, heading to the barn. It took her a few minutes to make her legs move to go back to the house. But once started she grabbed her skirt and began running. She didn't stop until she was inside and the door closed behind her.

It took all her will power to turn and watch for him and Michael to ride out of the yard. "I hope you are right Levi." She turned the lock in the door once they were out of sight and walked through the house to lock the other door as he wanted her to do.

"I'm a big girl." She bit at her nail and wondered why she sounded like a ten year old.

"Alone for a couple days, I should survive without you, I hope." She closed her eyes over the avalanche of feelings filling her because of his absence and it had only been a little while since they left. She realized her worry rested in what Levi said he decided about Michael. That he would tell Michael everything while they were out to catch Lady left her a nervous wreck. Levi figured it would be the only way to be fair to Michael. "Not everything..."

The letter is what Levi would tell Michael about. Everything he could tell him without the time travel part is what Levi decided. Only Sally wasn't sure how he would do that without telling Michael all of it. "Just stay safe, Levi."

Chapter 9
Truth the hard way

Michael waited for Hooper to flush Lady out of the herd. The rope in his hand felt right, and he was ready when the mare swung out from the group. His heals dug into his horse, and they took out after Lady. Michael could hear the furious call from Diablo coming from up on the rise, he knew what they were doing.

He was glad he picked the fastest horse they had as they raced after Lady. His arm automatically came back to twirl the rope around before letting it fly out to capture the mare. "Yes!"

He pulled back to slow them all, glad that Lady didn't fight the rope, he didn't want her hurt in any way. As they finally came to a stop, both horses and Michael were out of breath. He quickly pulled in the extra rope and secured his hold about the saddle horn. His horse moved back to bring the rope tense to stop Lady from struggling.

Michael heard Hooper riding carefully up behind him. "She's doing good, Hooper."

"I saw how fast you caught her and calmed her down, great work Michael. I'm going to walk up and secure the halter and lead."

"Go ahead, I've got a good hold on her. Be careful, she's been out here a long time." Michael did worry that his mare had reverted back to her wild stage.

"Easy there girl."

He watched as Hooper brought out an apple for the mare. Michael figured another lady's hand was behind that treat. Hooper slid the halter on the mare as she chewed away. "You really are a lady's man, Hooper."

The man's smile said it all and Michael couldn't silence his laughter.

Levi walked up to his friend and handed him the mare's lead. "You just make sure you don't lose her. We've been chasing her for days."

"Order noted."

Michael finally got his humor under control and moved his horse out with the mare to follow Hooper. Yes, they did chase Lady and Diablo's herd for the last three days. Much longer than Hooper planned and he knew, his friend was impatient to get back to his wife.

"At least now I understand why he's so protective." Oh yes, Michael learned a lot these last days and he smiled, glad that Hooper trusted him. The tension between them was gone now and the relief felt wonderful. Michael knew he was relieved that both Hooper and Sally would be staying at the ranch. The fact that Hooper owned half of Twin Creeks and had these last two years eased Michael's worry. He knew how much work the man put into this place and neither of them wanted to lose it.

The foundation of the new house, barn and bunkhouse should be completed this week. They would start on the walls next. They would need to hire some extra hands to help with the cattle, once they cut out the half to sell this year.

"Hooper, how many men do we have that can break horses?"

"Ten besides you and me. We should be fine, even if someone gets hurt." He looked over at his friend and saw him smiling again. He did the right thing by telling Michael what was in the letter. "That devil sure did gather up a lot of mares. That is a huge herd, more than we figured."

"We will have to leave him with enough mares so he doesn't decide to go looking for more and find a way to leave with them."

"I did think about fencing off the entrance to the valley."

"Maybe after the building is finished, Hooper. She did say we had until next spring?"

"A year, yup, that's what she said."

"We should make it."

Hooper smiled over at Michael, "we will make it." He dug his heels in and eased into an easy lope. Looking back he made sure Lady was doing okay. "Let's show the big guy we are leaving with her."

"Time for the parade?"

"Oh yeah."

Together they rode towards the herd and one very angry stallion. As they hoped Lady put her two-cents in the mix the nearer they came to the herd.

Michael and Hooper turned away not wanting to get too close, but slowed enough to be sure that he followed. When they saw the stallion turning the herd to follow them, they both cheered and started riding towards home and the corral waiting for the herd.

As Hooper hoped the mares close to foaling drifted away from the main herd as did those with new colts. Without them the corral should be big enough. The closer they rode to the ranch the more anxious he was to see Sally. Now that things were settled between him and Michael, Levi felt a lot better. He realized Sally gave up her dream to find Angie for him, but they both knew it was the right decision.

"We should make it to the ranch before sundown."

"Once we get the herd inside we are going to need to get Diablo out of the corral. He'll bust out of it if we don't."

"I'll get a few men working on that, Hooper. You need to see to Sally."

Hooper nodded in agreement, looking back at the herd on their heels. "The overflow can be kept in the yard."

"I'll get the Reverend to close it up."

Hooper urged them into a little faster pace not wanting to lose the distance between them and Diablo. He wouldn't put it past the devil to fight them for Lady on the run. "Just keep your herd together big guy." The stallion was racing all around the herd, he was always in a different place when Hooper looked for him over his shoulder.

"Hooper! Is that..." Michael didn't need to finish his question. Hooper saw her at the same time he did. He looked back at the herd and knew there was no way to slow them down. "Just reach her in time, Hooper."

⟨≈⟩

The day truly was beautiful and Sally decided to try and enjoy it, though she missed Levi. They'd been gone three days now, and she hoped he would return today.

"He loves me, he loves me not, what a silly thing to be doing," she said as she tossed the daisy petal down and then tossed away what was left of the daisy. "I know he loves me, I don't need a silly kid's game."

Sally smiled to herself and picked some more flowers for the bouquet. The house was spotless, she wanted the flowers for the kitchen and main room. She'd cleaned up their room and redecorated a wee bit. "He'll like it."

Saying the words didn't make it so and she sighed. "I hope he will at least try to like it." To say both their lives changed these last weeks was mild.

One thing she was sure of, "I've never been happier." Odd how every day she felt more at home. Of course Levi had a lot to do with her acceptance. She refused to think of life here or anywhere without him in hers.

The possibility brought back the troubling thoughts from yesterday. The two men that rode into the ranch had immediately drawn her attention. Sally remembered she finished hanging up the last of the washed curtains. She rarely ventured beyond the house and yard, but something, maybe their dark, long coats and bowler hats, drew her attention. The men too seemed to feel the darkness of these two for they all gathered around and it wasn't in welcome. The Reverend moved forward and confronted the two riders that didn't dismount from their horses. Sally remembered seeing many of the men fingering their guns and some carried rifles.

"What brings you two out this far?" The Reverend wasn't a man to ignore in any situation.

Sally could feel the riders looking at her; she refused to make eye contact and was glad when their attention was called away.

"We've been riding a far spell."

"No doubt, why here?"

Sally watched the Reverend spit after he asked the question again. It seemed a long time passed before one of the men answered.

"We're looking for a man, a Captain Hooper."

Sally stopped breathing, her heart pounded in her ears as fear swept through her. She realized these men weren't looking up an old friend. Oh no, they meant to hurt Levi, and she felt the rush of anger rise up inside her. The Reverend stepped forward and answered before Sally could move, and the young man named Jenkins moved in front of her. She instinctively knew he or any of them would prevent her from confronting the riders.

"Don't rightly know a Captain by any name out this way. You boys made a long ride for nothing."

Heads nodded in agreement with the Reverend through the crowd of men, and she saw the men take it all in. Again their attention rested on her. Another of the ranch hands deliberately moved to stand in front of her to end their direct view.

"If you do hear of him, there's a reward involved for bringing him to us."

"Long time since the war boys, what could anyone want with a Captain?"

"This Captain killed a man after the war and his family wants restitution for the deed."

"Family, not the court?"

"It's a private matter."

"Not round here, you just made it public." The Reverend took his hat off and looked up at them. "Best be heading out, town be a long way."

The man touched his hat, "We will be around for a couple weeks."

With that the two men turned and rode out. A couple of the hands mounted and followed them out.

Sally stood there, she felt sure her lip was bleeding from the pressure her teeth gave it to remain silent. The Reverend walked over to her as the men began moving away.

"You best warn Levi about this. The men won't say anything to them bounty hunters, but I doubt if they will be far from the ranch for a while."

Sally couldn't help but ask. "Do you know why they want Levi?"

"Aint none of my business, things happen in a man's life that are best left alone. The Captain is a good man, none finer, don't fret none your husband is safe."

"Thank you, Reverend."

Sally added another group of buttercups to her basket as she tried to push the memory away. "Trouble and all I've done is fret."

Bounty hunters in any time weren't something to be ignored. Levi told her little about his past, and she refused to pry. She loved the man he was right now, not the stranger he used to be. "No one will touch him."

All of a sudden Sally felt a shiver move up her legs, "oh, what the..." She realized the ground was trembling. She spun about trying to find the cause when her frantic gaze froze on the huge cloud of dust growing behind her. "It's coming this way...oh no—the horses!"

Sally didn't wait to see if her assumption was right she grabbed hold of her skirts and started running, the basket long forgotten over the panic flooding through her. She could hear them now, the thundering hooves!

She needed to reach the barn, it was the closest building; they would overtake her before she made it much farther.

"Sally!"

She turned to see if it was Levi and nearly stumbled.

Levi leaned down and grabbed hold of her praying he didn't drop her before pulling her onto the horse in front him. He held her between his arms and felt her own take hold and wrapped around to his back. He whipped the horse to keep him running as the first of the herd caught up with them.

Sally buried her head into his shoulders and held on; the horses were all around them. Running and bucking, moving every which way, she felt sure they were going to fall. She ground her teeth down in order not to scream.

"Hang on darling, just keep hold and don't look." He was yelling to her above the noise. "We need to keep moving with them toward the corral, I'll pull away by then."

She could nod into his shoulder too frightened to talk and refusing to look up.

Levi worked the horse through the herd to get to the outside, until finally they broke away, and he gradually slowed the horse down. He stopped them up on a rise and out of the mass of horses now inside the corral. He could see Michael directing the men to close off the entrance. His hand went to her hair, and he hugged her closer. "It is alright now Sally."

"The ground is still rumbling..."

His eyes closed as he fought down the fear that drove him to reach her in time. Feeling her in his arms made him suck in his breath in relief. His lips kissed her lovely head, thankful she was safe. "Sally, I'm so sorry, my dear, sweet wife."

Levi's arms tightened around her and wished he could protect her all the time. "They are settling down now. It is really something to see so many."

He smiled down at her when she finally pushed herself up to see. "Wow, it is breathtaking, Levi."

"I'm sure glad we made the corral big enough."

They both let the nervous giggle break through and take away the fear that gripped them.

Levi's fingers brushed her hair out of her face. "Now the work begins."

Sally looked up at him, "I'm really glad you are back and safe, I missed you so much."

Her words penetrated his concentration on her hair. "I missed you too, lady."

Her arms tightened about him over the flash of fear he failed to hide from her. "I...you are my life Levi Hooper."

His lips touched hers with a wisp of awe before he deepened the kiss. He didn't care what anyone saw or thought Levi embraced the woman in his life with a fever that wouldn't be tamed.

When he finally pulled back he looked into her beautiful eyes and smiled. "You are a wonder, Sally, a beautiful woman that has stolen my heart."

Sally's laughter sang out as he turned his horse and rode out toward the woods. Her fingers worked to release the buttons on his shirt, and he urged the horse into a faster pace. She looked up and licked her lips over his sexy gaze. She heard his groan and pushed herself up against him to kiss his neck.

Her kisses felt like a hot iron across his flesh as her lips trailed down his neck to the open area she exposed of his chest. His hand tightened against her back not wanting her stop and fearing her adventurous loving would cause her to fall. Levi eyed the woods and felt they were far enough from the ranch to be safe, besides, Michael and boys had their hands full. He should feel guilty leaving, but he wouldn't be worth shit if he'd stayed. No, not the way she looked at him and made his blood boil.

Sally knew the horse stopped, but she didn't cease her discovery of his flesh. "Mmm, you do taste good my husband."

"You're wicked but oh so wonderful, Sally." Levi slid out of the saddle with her in his arms. He lowered her feet slowly to the ground as she moved over the evidence of her handiwork. "You are a hard woman to ignore."

"Never ignore me, Levi. I want you inside me." Her hand gripped the hard rod beneath his pants. "No, never that." She smiled against the heated groan he failed to keep silent as her other hand moved over his chest. "I'll never tire of feeling you."

Levi gripped her hips and pulled her tight against him, trapping her hand. "Come on, let's find a place to take this further."

She sighed over the release he sought then grinned and moved away from him as he undid his bedroll.

"There's a nice place over this way. He took hold of her hand and pulled her after him, impatient to reach the spot he wanted to show her.

Sally heard the water before they stepped out of the trees. "Oh my, Levi, it is beautiful."

The waterfall captured her attention until he came up behind her and pressed into her back. "Mmm, that feels so good, I missed you so much." She leaned harder against him, deliberately moving her backside over his hard-on.

His lips were hot against her neck and Sally tipped her head to give him more to kiss. Her hands reached back and buried themselves in his thick hair. She loved to feel him, touch him... "Keeping you close to me, I want you to always be near me, Levi."

The touch of his arms moving over her shoulders drew a deep moan of need from her. His fingers worked her buttons open driving her crazy. She could feel how wet she was and grew more inpatient to have him ease the ache inside away. "I want you to drive that magnificent rod of yours deep inside me. Touch me where no other man will ever know. I am yours Levi, forever."

She closed her eyes when his powerful arms lifted her up and carried her to the bedding he put out. His lips here hot and wanting all she could give him. He took them both down onto the blanket and Sally pushed his shirt off so her hands could feel the power of her man. She came up on her knees as she worked to rid him of his pants. His hands rose to pull her clothes off.

Hot and wanton her lips moved over his chest and down his stomach, glorying in the tightening of his muscles, the ridges earned her apt attention. She couldn't get enough of him and her hands took hold of his erection, moving lovingly over the thick, throbbing length. The way his fingers played into her hair drove her crazy, making her hold tighten until Levi pulled her gently away.

Sally's protesting moan earned his knowing smile. "My turn, love." And Levi wasted no time discovery the treasure in his arms. He tasted himself on her lips surprised over the powerful need that took hold of him. She was his and Levi wanted all that was this woman. "My wife, so beautiful."

He heard her moan as his lips cherished her breasts taking the hard teats deep into his mouth. Like a starving man he suckled her, picturing how she would look carrying his child. The thought stunned Levi, but the possibility took hold of him, and he knew he never wanted anything as badly as having a child with Sally.

Determined to love her, his lips trailed over the satin length of her stomach to the furred entrance of her sex. Levi's hand covered the soft bush causing her to rise up and press into his palm. His name came soft and heavy from her lips. He held her sensual gaze with his own promise and Levi took his time lowering his lips to suckle her sexual heat. He worked his way to the core of her warm desire, holding Sally still for his pleasuring and Levi drove his woman hard and fast to an explosive climax.

Levi spread her thighs and moved up to give her exactly what she asked of him. He slid the head of his rod over her, spreading the moist heat around. Poised at the entrance of her velvet folds Levi waited for her to look into his gaze wanting her to see how much he wanted her. "Mine Sally, always and forever."

And Levi drove himself into her soft, giving flesh. She rose to meet him and hold him in that special place that only he could reach. It was some time before he began the dance of two lovers, soon the fire inside him ruled and Levi pounded against her willing flesh, holding nothing back. Their love making felt like a grand battle that each wanted, each waited forever to have and neither refused to gentle.

Their cries of fulfillment echoed through the forest drowning out the roar of the waterfall!

⚜

Sally settled against Levi's shoulder as he pulled her closer. She smiled knowing neither of them wanted the other to stray. Her finger moved over his chest, and he huffed beneath her. "You turn me on, Levi Hooper."

"Let me catch my breath, darling."

She laughed softly against his shoulder, making him squirm. Sally looked up at him and returned his sexy smile. When she pushed off of him she held his gaze and backed away. She looked back at him laying there with his head propped up watching her. She reached the water edge and smiled at him, beckoning him to join her as she walked into the cool lake.

Each stroke took her farther out in the lake, she heard his long strokes, and she turned over on her back to meet him as he joined her in the middle of the lake. "Feels good, Levi."

"I don't think it will cool me down any."

Her laughter joined his as they swam around each other, fingers moving over their slick bodies. Sally went under to wet her hair and before coming up her lips kissed the head of his hard member. When she broke the surface, his arms were waiting to gather her to him. Her legs went about his waist. "I love this place, thank you for bringing me here."

His eyebrow rose and he smiled. "Just don't come this far from the ranch on your own, there are still some Indians about these parts."

"And other two legged no goods." The words brought her troubling thoughts back and Sally slid out of his arms and swam to shore, knowing she needed to talk to him.

She gathered up her dress and wrapped it about her as she sat on the bank and waited for him to join her.

"Okay, what's bothering you, Sally?"

She rested her head on her knees and turned to look at him. "Yesterday two bounty hunters rode into the ranch..."

Sally told him all that happened and what the Reverend said. "He came and told me that they are camped outside the ranch. So, I'm worried for you, Levi."

He pushed away and started getting dressed. She noticed that he checked his guns before putting on his shirt. She quickly dressed and wished she didn't need to tell him something like this and ruin the day.

Levi's finger came under her chin to raise her face. "It's alright Sally."

"Is it, Levi? They want you and I don't think they care how they get you."

He pulled her into his embrace and rested his chin on her head. He hated having to tell her about the time he wanted to forget. "I was married to a girl before the war started." His lips kissed the top of her head and his arms kept her against him, refusing to let her move away. "When the war ended I went home, only I wasn't welcomed any longer. Seems she got tired of waiting for me and up and married someone else, a Randy Black." He sighed over the ugly memory of that day. "Problem was I survived the war and Randy decided I should have died."

"Oh Levi, how awful for you."

"He called me out on the main street with a lot of witnesses. I only wounded him when he drew on me. I started to walk away when someone shouted out a warning...that stupid man drew on me again...I had no choice but to shoot."

She held him close, trying to soothe the pain she heard inside of him.

"There was a trial, people came forward and told the judge what happened and I was set free. The judge ruled self-defense."

"Then it is his family that sent these men?"

His hand cupped her face, "yes, I guess we can't escape our past."

"What can you do?" Sally could feel the fear filling her for Levi.

"I won't go with them." Levi said each word slowly as he held Sally.

Chapter 10
Moving Forward

Sally's fingers gripped the fence board, swallowing the scream she wanted to give into as Levi moved past her on the bucking horse. The men cheering for the rider echoed in her head. She wanted to yell at all of them. Breaking horses was too dangerous, and she wished Levi would stop.

"He's the best there is with the horses." Michael settled into his seat on the fence beside her. His gaze drifted down the white knuckle hold she maintained on the fence. "Sally, he is alright. Hooper knows when to get away from the bad ones."

Under her breath, for she feared all the emotions racing through her would explode, "he could get hurt really bad doing this."

Michael looked away from her imploring gaze. "Yeah, guess he could, but he hasn't been hurt yet." He wanted to tell her that his friend needed to do this to keep himself from confronting those damn bounty hunters still camped outside the ranch.

"Taking these chances won't make them go away."

His gaze jutted up to hers, "No, but it is better than the alternative."

Her teeth raked her bottom lip over the concern from Levi's friend. She weighed his words and sighed, "Yes, you are right, it is better, but this is one hell of an alternative."

It was Michael's turn to be shocked. "Don't ever change, Sally. I'd miss the attitude." His laughter almost made him fall off the fence, finally earning a smile from Sally.

Their attention went back to Levi now riding out the last of the bucking from the pretty appaloosa. Sally smiled and waved to Levi. "She will have a fine colt. I hope he has a full blanket."

"You know horses."

"Angie and I rode a lot as kids. I haven't done much of it since."

"Levi wants to keep this mare."

She smiled, "Really? I'm glad, it would be wonderful to have her bloodlines with Diablo. She's a beautiful appaloosa and probably came from the original Spanish horses, she's got a lot of Arab in her, just like Diablo."

Sally turned and saw Michael staring at her in wonder. "Yes, I do know horses." She laughed at the way he finally shut his mouth.

"No kidding."

Levi walked up to them and couldn't help but ask, "What's got you two all riled up?"

Michael answered, "Did you know your wife knows horse blood lines."

Levi smiled, "Sally knows horses, guess I forgot to mention that."

They all three laughed and Sally realized it was the first she'd seen Levi smile since that day. Neither of them spoke of it again, but he did begin to tell her about his life before the war and after, especially about the cattle drive to here. Sally remembered how hard she laughed when he told her about how Angie held those guns on the rustlers. Oh yes, her friend made a huge impression on Levi.

Michael's question made her bring her attention back to them.

He asked her, "Would you like to start an accounting of the mares, maybe by breed and the colts. Just on the ones we are going to keep to start our line."

She looked at Levi and his slight nod of acceptance, funny how she never wanted anyone's permission before. It wasn't really permission, more like she wanted to know he agreed. "I'd like to do that Michael. I think it would be very important to know and have a starting point."

"Diablo is certainly doing his part." They all looked over at the stallion racing about in his pen. The high stud pen fence kept him from jumping out, but Sally noticed he was starting to dig out and told Michael and Levi about it this morning. The hole was filled and new logs had been rolled over and braced against the bottom fence rail.

"Do you think he will find a way out?"

"We are going to have release him soon." Levi's arm came about her shoulders when he straddled the fence and another man took up breaking the horses. "Once we get the mares together we will let them all go back to the valley."

"The new fence across the entrance should be finished today. That will help keep him here."

Michael didn't have to say that it would keep certain bounty hunters out.

Since the two of them returned with the herd, there'd been a new easiness with Michael that Sally was glad to experience. Levi told her what he told Michael, and she could hear the man's own pleasure over the tension between them *all* being gone. Sally decided that giving up looking for Angie was the right decision. She figured Angie took Striker to Canada, yes; it would be the safest place to go.

"A penny for your thoughts, Sally?"

She smiled up at Levi, "just clearing out things."

He leaned closer and whispered beneath the cheering men for the bronc' rider. "Things like Angie?"

She nodded, "I figure she went to Canada."

"Why there?"

"Safer than here and it is where I would go."

With that he smiled, "smart lady."

"Yes, she is that."

"So is her friend." With that Levi let the conversation end, he didn't want Michael to get wind of it and stir up those thoughts again. He hugged Sally closer, feeling the tightness in his chest ease. He'd told her a lot about his past these last days. He worried how she would react over his marriage. She surprised him last night by telling him *she married the Levi Hooper of now and all those things in the past made him a better man today.*

Hooper would always remember her words. They were the only thing she had to say about his past or the war, except for humor over the ruckus Angie caused. In truth, he would love to see those two together. He could imagine the two of them plotting some deed or another. "Maybe someday, Sally."

The squeeze of her hand on his thigh said she knew exactly what he meant.

Sally walked around the frame of the new house surveying all the progress. The walls and roof were on the house and the bunkhouse. They planned on raising the barn walls and roof this week and the men were all excited about it.

Michael had the men dismantling the barn below so they could use the wood planks that were good up here, to save time and expense. Sally told him he was *recycling,* and she thought his mouth would never close. He told Levi that she came out with a lot of new thoughts, like Angie.

She smiled and kept walking knowing Levi shared their secret with Michael. Levi's friend would never say anything, and she pretended not to know that he knew where she came from. Sally felt her slips only confirmed for him of just how far she did travel to get here.

Her hand moved over the window framed in Levi and her bedroom. She could overlook the whole valley from here. She liked the layout of the house and couldn't wait for it to be ready to move in. The whole house was actually designed as two houses in one. The downstairs consisted of two living areas on each side with the kitchen in the middle and one great room for a central living area in front of the kitchen wall and a glassed in area like a green house off the kitchen for a dining area. Sally loved this area. Levi told her it would keep her from watching the snow. She laughed all afternoon about his insight. There were three smaller rooms downstairs toward the back of the house. Sally felt at least one should be used for the ranch office.

Michael was actually the one that came up with the design. He surprised Levi and her, telling them that it would work out so they each could have a house for their family. Sally walked up and hugged the man. Levi's friend was a very special person.

As she made her way downstairs Sally remembered how Levi insisted that there be a pantry for the food stocks. That addition came after she asked him to go into the cellar for some potatoes for dinner. He nearly slid off the steps and over the side. "I think he got the point." Sally smiled, knowing he did when he told her to let him know what she needed from the cellar, and he would get it from now on. There would be a cellar here in the new house, but one with a much better design and safer stairs. She peaked at the walled hole and stair outline of the cellar. "Darn I hate those things."

There were six bedrooms upstairs, two master bedrooms with four between them. Sally drifted in thought over the rooms as her gaze rose back to the upstairs. "Fill them all..." those were Levi's words to her when she asked why there were so many. "Mister impatient is what he is."

Her soft laughter floated on the summer breeze as her hand absently moved over her stomach. The action stopped when she realized what she was doing. "Am I?" Sally wished she knew more about being pregnant, but it wasn't like she took a course in it. She wondered if Levi would know, but Sally brushed the thought away.

She turned in a circle and smiled over the progress of the house. They would be leaving soon to take the horses to the military and then the cattle drive to Miles City and the railway. Sally wanted to go to the town and hoped Levi would let her come. There were many things she needed for the new house, she already had a list started.

"And no man is going to pick the material for my curtains." She sighed, "at least it will be ready in time." The relief slid through her over the fact the whole ranch would be moved up to the plateau before the flood she read about happened. She asked Levi if the horse herd and cattle would be safe, he told her the horses were smart enough to move to higher ground and as the flood would be in the spring they should all be farther back and away from the area the melt off of snow would come down and then into the valley. Michael and Levi road the length of the creek that they figured would turn into the raging river and felt sure the animals would survive.

"Now the people will as well."

Sally stepped out onto the porch to take in the magnificent view. She could see the whole ranch. Diablo and Lady were free now with the rest of the mares Levi and Michael handpicked for the breeding. There were still enough for the contract with the military next year.

To her surprise Levi told her the appaloosa mare was hers. Her gaze went to the beautiful horse tied up to the hitch rail out in front of the house. She loved having the mare that she named Beauty. She tried to ride every day, Sally was always careful to stay in sight of the ranch because of her promise to Levi.

Her teeth ground over the trouble still camped outside the ranch fence. Those two men were stayed there, waiting. "It's been over a month now." She closed her eyes for a second and wished they would give up and leave.

All the men wore their guns now because of the threat the bounty hunters posed. Sally worried for Levi. She knew how much he hated using the guns, but she wasn't foolish enough to think he wouldn't shoot if he must, to survive.

She looked at the sun's position and knew she should head back down. Beauty perked up as Sally walked over to her. "Easy pretty Beauty, you are still jumpy over being ridden," she pulled herself up into the saddle, "I can't blame you." Her hand patted Beauty's sleek neck, to calm her down before moving her out. Just as she turned the horse she saw two riders coming towards the ranch. "Damn them."

Her heels dug into the Beauty and sent her racing down the road to reach the ranch ahead of the riders. Her frightened gaze searched the yard for Levi as she galloped in. "There, by the barn. Come on Beauty, we can warn him."

She pulled back hard on the reins to stop the horse.

Hooper came instantly alert to the racing rider and horse coming at him. That Sally was riding like a wild woman sent his alarms alive.

"Whoa there girl," Hooper grabbed the rearing horse's reins to help Sally get her under control. "What's wrong Sally?"

"Bounty hunters are riding this way!" Sally kicked out of the stirrups and slid to the ground. "I could see them riding in, Levi."

"Take Beauty and go to the barn." Hooper's stoned gaze went beyond her to the riders. He noted that the other men were moving his way. "Go on Sally, I don't want you anywhere near this."

She wanted to argue, but realized his attention would be on her if she stayed, and he needed to focus on the danger now in sight. "I'll stay in the barn, Levi."

He nodded without looking at her and Sally forced herself to move with Beauty. She made it inside the barn and out of sight as the two riders pulled to a halt in front of Levi and the men with him.

Sally tied Beauty off and went to the tack-shed, her trembling hand lifted the rifle off the rack. "I do know rifles, my dear husband." She moved quietly back to the barn entrance but stayed in the shadows. She cocked the rifle and brought it to her shoulder, ready for what might come. All thoughts of the danger to Levi pounded in her head, she took a deep breath to hold the fear back and concentrate on what was being said.

"I asked you what you want here." Levi's voice echoed under his suppressed raged.

"We've come for you, Captain Hooper."

Sally fought back the tears that threatened to fall. Her attention flew to Levi over the man's announcement.

"Then you have a problem. The courts cleared me of any charges, it was self-defense. I've no intention of going anywhere with you."

The two men didn't say anything for a while, but Sally could see the smirk that came over one of them. Under her breath, "go away, go now."

"The problem is yours, Captain. We aren't leaving until you go with us."

"Then I hope you brought a lot of supplies."

The tension flying between the men and Levi was almost a living thing and Sally feared what might come.

Levi stepped towards them, "turn your horses and move out or dismount and we will settle it."

The one man that seemed to speak for both of them leaned forward over the saddle horn towards Levi. Sally's finger tightened on the trigger, the rifle barrel came up a notch as she took aim. "You will go..."

The shot that rang out, surprising everyone at once. The rider's hat flew up in the air and before it landed it was hit again with another shot. Levi sucked in his breath over exactly who he felt shot the bowler hat threw with bullet holes. He cursed softly but kept his attention on the two men. The one's whose hat was missing turned as white as a ghost. "I think that was a warning you might want to take seriously Frazier."

Yes, Levi knew the man. He wondered why Frazier would be doing this.

"You will pay for this, Hooper!" The man's words held more fear than threat as the two of them started to ride off.

Levi caught the movement of Sally's dress at the barn door and saw her take aim again. "No way, Sally." His growled curse followed him to reach her, but the rifle let loose before he could grab the gun. He turned to see the other hat fly off the rider's head. "Damn! She sure can shoot."

All the men turned to look at her, Levi saw her lower the rifle and look at him before turning and going back inside of the barn.

He called out orders for two men to follow them and make sure they stayed outside the ranch's fenced boundary. Levi's long strides reached the barn. It took a moment for his eyes to adjust to the dark interior. He saw her pulling the saddle from Beauty and picking up the brush, the rifle was back in the tack room on the wall rack. Levi walked over and the look she gave him said loud and clear to keep his distance. "I never gave you rifle lessons."

"Didn't have to." Sally started brushing down Beauty.

"I can see that and I think those two know it as well."

"They don't belong here."

Levi could hear the rage that drove her to shoot those hats off, ringing in her words. He leaned on the fence and watched her take out her anger with each lengthened stroke. The realization that she did this to defend him struck hard and fast. "I don't think they will be back."

"They better not." She felt him behind her and her hand slowed. "I'm sorry, Levi, but I couldn't stand it any longer."

His hand covered hers and took the brush away. "It's alright Sally, just take a deep breath." Levi pulled her back into his embrace ignoring her slight protest. He leaned down and placed his cheek to hers. "You're a damn good shot, Mrs. Hooper."

A slight smile came over her, "I used to shoot skeet a lot."

"Hmm, not sure what that is, but you must have been damn good at it." His lips brushed her sensitive ear earning a soft moan from her.

"I was, took last year's award for the best shooting."

Sally moaned when he smothered his humor against the bottom of her neck. The heat seemed to race through her and Sally felt her instant response. She rubbed her head against his, "I want you, Levi."

He groaned, "Let's go to the house, Sally. There are too many eyes here."

⚬⚬⚬

"I said no!"

"Damn it all, Levi. I need to go and I don't want to stay here without you. Not this time." She'd stayed here, under protest, when he drove the horses to the fort. Michael was here that time, but neither of them would be with her this time.

He turned in time to catch her shoulders and hold her still. "It is too dangerous."

"Oh really, and how dangerous is it for me to be here alone with hardly anyone around?" She glared up at him. "Hmm, what's the matter? No answer for that one? Well, I have one, it would damn dangerous if those two creeps don't follow you and the cattle."

His jaw hardened over her argument, one that he'd faced the last couple of days. Even Michael told him to let her come. "You don't know how hard it is."

"If Angie survived it I sure can."

Hooper's gaze drifted to her stomach. "She wasn't carrying a child."

He felt her sway in his hold. "Sally?"

Her enlarged eyes stared at him a moment. In breathless wonderment she asked. "Really? Am I pregnant, Levi?"

He couldn't stand it and pulled her to him, his hand cupped her head to his chest. "I think you are, Sally."

Levi didn't stop her from pulling back and looking up at him. "How do you know if I am?"

His thoughts stumbled for a second, realizing she honestly didn't know. "Sally, didn't anyone, your mother maybe, talk to you about these things?"

Her head slowly shook, "no, I'm sorry I just don't know..."

"Hey, it is okay, we will be fine." He pulled her back into his arms. "You haven't had a womanly time of month for a long time, two months at least."

"You're right, I haven't, but I wasn't sure that was all I needed to know."

"And your breasts are fuller and tender."

She turned her face into his shoulder and sighed. "Now that's the truth."

Sally moved back and looked up at him, "Are you happy about this, Levi?"

"Lady, I've never wanted anything so much in my life." He smiled down into her amazing gaze. His fingers combed back the long lengths of her hair from her face. "I don't want you to get hurt out there on the trail, Sally."

"I can ride."

"Yes, you can and as good as Angie could. What did you two do—teach each other?"

She laughed softly over his teasing question. "No, we just did everything together. Neither of us had parents, so we stuck together on everything. Except the shooting, I did that when she was away at school." His lips felt so right on her brow, but Sally knew this wasn't finished. "Levi, I honestly don't want to stay here without you. I can ride and I'll take it easy, I promise not to overdo it." She wanted to remind him that she rode nearly every day around here.

"Something could happen, Sally. I don't want you or the baby hurt."

She refused to look away from his stony glare. "Promise me you will think about me going? Please, Levi?"

He lowered his head and she waited for his answer.

"If it weren't for the baby and how rough this drive will be, I'd say yes. But Sally, I know what can happen out there, but I will think about it."

She gave him a smile, "thank you. I won't fight you on this, but I do hope you will let me come with you."

Levi kissed her and then walked away. He was out the door before he let out his breath. "We are going to have a child!"

Sally heard his yell from the kitchen door and laughed. Her hand went over her stomach. "Wow. He's really excited—so am I, little one, so am I."

She went about the morning chores with a smile permanently etched on her face. "Oh my!" Sally rushed into the other room and pulled her shopping list from the desk drawer. "I'll need yarn and more material, bottles, a crochet needle—I was never any good at knitting." Her brow furrowed, "not sure how good I am with crocheting either, but it did seem easier, shoot, I'll figure it out..."

"What will you figure out?"

She turned with her list in hand, "Hi Levi."

"What is there to figure out, Sally?"

She finally looked up at him, "oh, the crocheting, I need to figure out how to do it. I tried it once, but it was never something I liked much."

Levi relaxed, glad she was too busy with her list to realize how upset he got. He silently berated himself for doubting her and wondered why he would think she was planning anything. He sighed, it was the whole baby thing. Levi never expected something so small to affect him much. "You can go." He held up his hand when she spun about. "Only, I don't want you riding anything. You can ride on the wagon."

She wanted to protest that the wagon was worse than a horse, but she knew that stance of his. "Thank you, Levi." Sally smiled, "I will ride on the wagon."

She was too happy not to walk up to him and kiss him. "We will be fine. I need so many things for the baby! Do you know, I have no idea what all I need, I'm guessing." Her laughter finally eased his stance against her. "If you think of anything I need to get please tell me." She looked up into his softer eyes, "I need your help, Levi. I've never had a baby before."

He huffed, "neither have I."

"I guess we will figure it out together." She gave him a quick kiss before moving back. "I want you with me when I have the baby."

With that she moved away and started on her list again. Levi watched her walk up the stairs before disappearing. "Guess I better find out how to bring that baby into the world."

Chapter 11
Finding the Way

"Whoa there!" Bob pulled up the team just time for the missus to lean over the side and empty her stomach again. "No more greasy bacon for you."

She accepted the rag he passed her to wipe her mouth. "I'd argue, but I don't have enough energy left."

"You'd best be finding some, your husband is riding over."

Sally wanted to cry over how rotten she felt, but letting Levi see was forbidden. They were two days away from the ranch and slow as the cattle were, she figured he could take her back in a day. She forced herself to sit up and blaster a smile on her face as he pulled his horse to a halt.

"Why did you stop again, Bob? Sally?" Damn it, he knew this was a bad idea. She looked pale he wondered how she managed to sit there and not fall over.

Her hand came out to grip Bob's arm halting his answer. "I am just having some morning sickness because of the baby. Bob was nice enough to slow down for me."

Levi knew exactly what she meant, this 'morning sickness' as she called it started a week before the drive. "It's nearly mid noon, you'd best tell the little guy to get with it."

With that announcement Levi yanked his horse around and rode off.

Bob snickered over his leave. Sally sucked her breath in, "guess we better get moving."

The man clicked the reins and moved the team out not saying a word until they rode a while. "I 'aint one to pry Missus, but are you sure you shouldn't let him take you back?"

Sally knew the whole drive heard their yelling match last night. Levi's insistent belief she needed to go home started the first morning on the drive. "No, I need to be here."

"Yup, you are just as stubborn as your friend."

If she didn't feel so darn sick she would have laughed over his conclusion. Maybe Levi was right and she should go home. But thinking about it made her angry. "I'd be worse there then here."

"Then you'd best go in the back and lie down. Seems to me the babe needs to get used to the rock'n of the wagon. You should be better in a day or so."

Sally started to move back, she stopped and smiled at Bob. "I sure hope the baby heard that, Bob. Personally, I think I'd be better off on Beauty."

She hit the cot and groaned over the dizziness that started rolling through her. Her hand came to rest on the mound of the baby that started showing his presence these last couple weeks. "Did you hear Bob, you need to get used to this swaying, argh, not that I blame you, sweetie." Sally closed her eyes.

A smile came over her as she rested in the back of the wagon. She tried to concentrate on the shopping she needed to get done and not the constant swaying. Not even going over all the various sewing projects for the baby and house could override the wagon's constant rocking. Levi's voice broke through her tired thoughts, and she sat up when the wagon stopped. "Levi?"

The back flap spread open, and he stood there not sure who he was angrier with. "Come on Sally, this is not working..."

"Levi, I'll be fine..."

"No you won't, but I'll be damned if you will stay in there, get out here and on Beauty."

"Really?" She moved towards him and smiled down at him when his strong hands lifted her out of the wagon.

"Yes darn it, but so help me Sally, if this doesn't work, you are going home."

She knew he was right. "I know, Levi."

With his nod he lowered her feet to the ground and handed her the reins. "Come on, let me help you mount."

She didn't argue, but refused to admit how weak she felt. Being off that swaying wagon immediately helped her feel better.

Bob started moving the wagon out, they waved him off.

Sally could feel Levi's hard stare watching her every move. "I'm okay, Levi, honest. It was the swaying of the wagon, it just made it all worse."

"I can agree it didn't help. Let's just see how you do on Beauty for the rest of the day."

He asked her to remain near him when they reached the cattle, and made her promise not to work the cattle. *Stay around the outside,* she smiled over his order. She didn't care what rules he made she was on Beauty and felt better.

Michael rode up to say hi to her. By the satisfied smile he gave Levi she figured out this was Michael's idea.

The rest of the day went by without incident and though she was tired she could have fell asleep on the horse, they both knew it was better than the wagon. Levi refused to let her help Bob with the meal, ordering her to go lie down in the wagon and rest. If she weren't feeling weak she would have argued, but it felt good to be still.

⚜

Michael joined Levi on the log with his dinner. "How is she?"

"Sleeping, I figured it would be better to let her sleep. She can eat latter."

"She seemed to do okay on the horse today."

Levi smirked, "Yeah, but you couldn't hear her when her promise stopped her from taking off after a cow."

"Seems I remember another lady like that." Michael's laughter joined Levi's.

"I just don't want anything to happen to her or the baby, Michael."

"I know, Levi, I'd feel the same way. But I think you are both better with her here than back at the ranch. You both would have worried yourselves sick."

Levi knew he was right, but he couldn't help but worry about her.

"Did you see them, Michael?"

"Yeah, they are following in our dust."

"I don't think they are going to stop."

"Probably not, just be sure you don't leave the herd, Levi. Stay close at all times."

Levi hated the danger those two men posed to everyone and especially to Sally. If he could have been certain they would follow and not stayed back when he left, he would have insisted she remain home. "Michael, if anything happens to me…"

"You don't have to say it. You know I'll take care of her and the baby."

"I know."

The two of them went back to discussing the cattle. Levi didn't want to think the worse, but neither could he ignore what might happen. He often wondered if he shouldn't have told Michael about how Sally actually came here. But now, with the bounty hunters after him, Levi knew it had been the right decision. She would be safe with Michael, they'd become best friends these last months.

His tense gaze went to the wagon. She seemed to be getting too ill over carrying the child. He hoped they would both survive the drive.

⚬⚜⚬

"Levi, I have my list." Sally held it up as if it were the answer to the world's problem.

"That's fine, but…"

"No buts, I came all this way to get these things for the house and baby and I'm going to do it." She gave him a small smile to take the bite out of her harsh declaration. "Now, go on and get those cattle sold, I'm not going anywhere but this store." She could add she was too damn tired to move any further, but she figured that wouldn't get Levi moving to leave her here.

He moved to her and wrapped his arms around her, heedless to the people that passed them. "If you feel dizzy…"

"I promise to sit on the first available spot." She leaned her head back to look up into his concerned gaze. Her hand rose to his rough cheek and she smiled. "It's a store, I'll be fine."

He could tell her that her friend thought she was fine in the wagon…he pushed the unpleasant thought away. "The cattle yard is at the end of this street."

"If I need you I'll send for you, I doubt I'm up to walking that much yet." Her short laugh didn't ease his hard stance. "You said yourself that they were gone, Levi."

"Yeah, but that doesn't mean much."

"I don't think they would be foolish enough to try anything here."

He looked around them, checking for those bounty hunters. "Maybe not."

"Please Levi, there are so many things I need to look for, I probably won't get this done before you and Michael are finished." Sally leaned closer and stood on tiptoe to whisper to him, "besides, I have never been in a store like this one and I can't wait to see it all."

He didn't hide from looking to the heavens for help, earning her soft laugh. She'd been so darn excited over coming into town and seeing everything, she badgered him most the night with questions about things she hoped to see and the prices of things. "Don't let them take your money, Mrs. Hooper."

She leaned back in his arms, "never happen, Mr. Hooper."

Sally met his descending lips with as much passion as his possessive kiss. More than one person walked by and giggled over the spectacle they made. Levi forced himself to pull back, he stared at the dreamy look on his wife's face and hoped it never disappeared. "Take care, Mrs. Hooper."

She smiled, turning in a neat circle to watch him walk away down the street. "You too, Mr. Hooper."

Sally sighed over the lightness in her heart for this special man. "He loves me." When he disappeared from sight she finally turned to go into the Emporium.

The store promised to be a marvelous adventure; one Sally looked forward to the whole drive. Her sweeping gaze couldn't take it all in. Levi told her the Emporium touted to be the largest in the west. "An early Wal-Mart." She laughed over the comparison.

She took a deep breath and picked an aisle to start down, there were many things to see she couldn't help picking one thing up after another. When she filled her arms she looked around and wondered what to do with it all.

"Here you go Missus," the man passed her a basket. "When you fill that bring it to the counter and I'll get you another."

"Thank you." she poured the items in her arms into the basket he held out for her.

"I'm Henry Billows, I own this store."

Sally smiled up at the tall thin man, "It is a marvelous place, Mr. Billows."

He returned her smile, "You just take your time and if you get tired there are chairs over there by the stove."

She nodded and he moved away. Sally laughed to herself and wondered if the man expected her to buy out the store. Her free hand moved over the baby she carried and whose evidence could now be seen beneath her dress. "I need material don't I."

The man's dark gaze followed the lady's progress through the store. He looked back at his partner and gave him a slight nod to his raised brow. Finally, one of them was alone. The woman wouldn't have been his first choice, but like Will said that man would do anything to protect her. Ben couldn't argue that point after watching the two of them these last weeks on the trail. Once they figured out which town they were headed to, Ben decided they might as well ride ahead and wait in comfort for the drive to arrive.

They'd taken turns watching for their arrival, Ben spotted the lady right off, and she wasn't one you would forget. His gaze went down to the swell of her child, and he ground his teeth over the thought of taking her without hurting her or the baby. He may catch men for money, but he wasn't a murderer and never did he harm a woman or child. He warned Will to be careful and that she was hands off. The woman was an ends to a means, nothing more. They would let her go once they had Hooper.

Seeing that Will was coming over, Ben moved out of the doorway in order not to be overheard.

His partner spoke under his breath. "Is she in there?"

"Shopping the store out, she's going to be a while." Ben looked around to make sure no one was near enough to hear them.

"We can't wait all day." Will hissed out.

Ben kept his voice calm. "No, but we can't take her in there, either."

"I've had enough waiting."

Will wasn't a man to rile, but Ben made the decisions in this. "We wait until she comes out."

Ben watched his partner move off in a huff. "The man needs more patience."

The reward would be worth the time they put into this one. Ten thousand dollars would set him up with the ranch he wanted, splitting it with Will. Of course that meant keeping Hooper alive, he wasn't worth anything dead.

Ben ground his teeth down over the truth of it. The man wasn't wanted by the law, but then Mr. Black had enough money to make his own laws. The one good thing Ben felt about this job is that there weren't any other hunters after the man. Or at least none that found him.

⟨⟨⟩⟩

"Yes that one please." She looked at her list, "I need four yards of that material."

"Are you planning to get all this sewing done before the child comes?"

The man was teasing her and Sally laughed. "Maybe, at least enough to move in."

"There you are Mrs. Hooper. Is there anything else?"

"You know, I think I will take 2 yards of that blue gingham."

"A right smart color that one."

"I'll be right back, I'll need thread for that one."

Sally knew where to find the color she needed. "One spindle should do it and another pack of needles to be safe."

Her hand reached out to grip the counter over the rush of dizziness that hit her. "Not now, I'm almost done." She hissed out the order and took some deep breaths. The room slowly came back to normal, she wondered if the whole pregnancy would be this way. She figured she started the fifth month and still she had morning sickness and dizzy spells.

Another steadying breath gave her the courage to let go of the counter. She shied away from looking at Mr. Billings, he'd seen her have an attack, and she knew he was watching.

Sally knew just what she needed and didn't look any farther. "There you go Mr. Billings, I think that is everything."

Sally acted like she was checking her list one last time. "Oh, I forgot one thing."

The man smiled at her, "What would that be?"

"I would love some of those liquorish sticks please."

He put half a dozen in a small bag and handed them to her. "Those are on me, I've never had so much fun filling an order."

"Why thank you, Mr. Billings, it has been wonderful shopping here."

The man worked on packing up her order into big boxes, he told her earlier he would hold them for her husband to pick up with the wagon. She mentally counted the barrels of nails and gunpowder Levi asked her to get, and the ropes Michael needed. It really was a huge order, none of them knew when they would get here again. "If you are ever out our way Mr. Billings please stop in and stay over."

"I'd be glad to do that, Mrs. Hooper."

Sally sucked on the candy stick as she watched him. "Would you mind if I wait over in the chair for Levi?"

"Not at all, you go right ahead."

Once she sat down, she closed her eyes over the relief flooding through her. She never realized how much extra energy it took to carry a child. Her hand lovingly moved over the mound that gave a couple kicks as if it felt her hand. "Get strong little one, there is this whole, wonderful world waiting for you."

❧

H e wet the pencil's tip on his tongue and put the last letter down on the paper. Ben folded it and placed it in the envelope. The shop owner was taking care of another customer and Ben waited for the older lady to leave, his gaze never left Mrs. Hooper. When she didn't come out, and he heard of her plan to wait there for Hooper, Ben decided to change the plan. He sure hoped Will was waiting with the horses.

He put the letter addressed to Hooper on the counter and drew out his gun. The man turned his way when he called him over. "I need you to give this letter to Mr. Hooper." Ben didn't give the man a chance to say anything before he showed his gun. "Now, move on back nice and easy, I'm not here to rob you."

He could feel the sweat rolling down his back, Ben didn't like being out in the open. "Mrs. Hooper!" He watched her body jump then straightens in the chair. "I need you to come over here, Mrs. Hooper." He cocked the gun at the storekeeper to make his point.

The woman rose and stepped towards him. Ben moved back from the counter and motioned for her to step in front of him. "Right there, now we are going to walk out of here real nice like. If you cause me any trouble I'll have to shoot someone, do you understand, Mrs. Hooper?"

"Y...yes."

"Good, and you..." he pointed the gun back at the man before lowering it before the woman, "you make sure her husband gets that note."

The man nodded.

Ben pulled the lady in front of him, the gun stuck against the middle of her back. "Now let's take it nice and slow."

She moved where his hold directed. Sally's frantic gaze raced around the street outside the store looking for Levi.

"Best not wish for him to show, not here." He jerked harder on her arm to keep her in front of him. Will waited at the edge of the store with the horses. "I know you can ride, so no games."

Sally mounted the horse he shoved her against, nearly falling off the other side over another round of dizzy spells.

"I said no games!" He hissed in her ear as he took a seat behind her.

"I'm not, I get dizzy, a lot."

Ben cursed then wrapped his arm around her swollen stomach before digging his heels into the horse. They raced down the street away from the cattle pens and out of town. He looked back once or twice to see if anyone followed and finally relaxed a bit when no one showed. They kept the horses running, he wanted to make the bluffs outside of town before dark. Her husband would show at the river, like the letter said.

Chapter 12
Dangerous paths

"No! Damn it, no!" Levi shook off the hands that tried to stop him from grabbing the storekeeper. "You let them take her!"

"He had a gun on your wife, I'm sorry, Mr. Hooper."

Levi's fist hit the building beside the man's head. He realized the man did what he had to. His other hand came to rest on Billings' shoulder for a second before Levi pushed away. The sheriff told him they rode out toward the north hills. The letter told him where they would meet. It took him a couple of minutes to get his anger under control.

He called Jenkins over and gave him orders to round up the men.

"Michael?"

"I'm here."

"I can't let them take her with us..."

"You can't give yourself up!"

Levi looked at his friend. "What choice do I have, Michael?"

No one had any answers for him. Levi knew what he needed to do, what he must do.

Michael grabbed his arm, "We can surround the place, and we can get there before them. Grey can get up in the rocks with his long gun. I'll take some of the men and be on the other side."

"They can't see you, any of you. It would be too dangerous for Sally."

"We will be under cover. You know they are going to cross the river there and head east."

"It's the only place to cross for a couple miles, figure that's why he picked it." Levi ran his hand over his face. "Gentleman Ben Frazier..."

Michael looked at Levi over the name he spoke. "It isn't him?"

"He signed his name. I recognized him at the ranch, Michael." Levi passed Michael the letter. "That son of a bitch!"

"He won't hurt her, Levi."

"Taking her hurt her." He couldn't keep his anger in. "He knows damn him, he testified at the trial!"

"I remember, his testimony helped to clear you of the charges."

It killed him to remember the man. Levi wondered if a stranger would make him feel worse or better. "Now, he does this...why, Michael?"

Michael shook his head, "money."

"I need to get Beauty for her."

Michael didn't follow him knowing his friend needed time to think it all through and get his anger under control. "Ben Frazier..." The man wasn't exactly a friend, but they knew of each other, grew up in the same area, and attended the same balls... "Fought in the same battles."

⚜

Sally refused to take the plate of beans the man tried to pass her. That he dropped it beside her in the dirt didn't surprise her. Will, yes, that was his name, he was an angry man and as mean as his looks upon her implied. She held no doubts the other one kept him away from her. Ben, yes that is the name the mean one called him. He is the man in charge. He'd been that to her all day.

Ruefully, she admitted that he treated her as a lady, except for the ride here. She unconsciously rubbed her stomach over the bruising from his rough hold on her. Sally stopped immediately when she realized he was watching her. She didn't want either man's attention, and she mustn't faint again. No, that was the last thing she wanted. Sally truly feared what they might do if she gave them any trouble.

Ben moved over to the woman and placed the cup of water down beside the plate of beans she still ignored. "You'd best eat some, might be sometime before another meal."

"I can't..." Though she barely managed to voice the truth in face of his scowl, she knew he heard her. Sally bit her lip and kept her gaze away from the man, figuring it was best not to confront him.

"Seems to me that babe of yours is giving you a rough time."

Without thought her arms covered the child from his gaze. "He will settle down, it is early yet."

Ben snorted over her defense of the unborn child before moving away. "Eat it lady, you are going to need it."

He tried, he couldn't do more than that. The fact the woman wasn't strong bothered him. He planned on leaving her out here for someone to find or for her to walk back to town. He thought the Captain would be easier to deal with if he didn't have to see her. Looking at her, he thought she was paler than after the ride here. Ben remembered how she fainted during the ride. He took a deep breath and decided to make the decision tomorrow.

He thought to himself and figured her husband's men wouldn't be far behind the Captain. He would have to leave her at the river. She should be fine, his men would find her soon enough.

Sally sucked in her breath over the man's study of her. She honestly didn't want to know what his thoughts might be. The fact she occupied them made fear race through her. She bit her bottom lip to keep it from quivering. She wanted Levi, but then wished he would never come, for that scared her more.

She stood up and both men came to their feet. The boss one walked towards her. Sally forced herself to face him, "I have to...you know."

The fact the man looked as embarrassed as she felt didn't ease her fears any.

"Over there, and don't be stupid."

"I won't as long as you two stay here."

He gave a quick nod, and she took it as his agreement. Being pregnant didn't help her and Sally rushed to the bushes he indicated. "I swear I better not get poison ivy or bitten by some damn snake!"

Ben shook his head over the lady's angry outburst. She was different. He didn't like how weak she was, but she possessed a surprising spunk, more than most women. The truth made him certain the man would show, alone, as instructed.

She came back and walked right past him as regally as a queen would. Ben fetched her a blanket for the night. He laid out his own bedroll a few feet from her, wanting to make sure Will kept his distance. The man would take the first watch, Ben didn't trust him with the late one.

Sally managed to lie down. Once things settled she turned on her side to watch the fire, trying to block out the men's presence. She didn't want to cry, but the tears rolled down her cheeks defying her attempts to stop them. She silently prayed that Levi wouldn't show at the meeting place. Squeezing her eyes shut she knew he would, knew he would give up just as Sally knew she would do whatever it took to keep their baby safe. The truth of the situation broke her heart.

Her hands covered their child under the blanket, and she tried to control her emotions. She felt sick and tried not to think about it.

⚬⚭⚬

B en raised his hand to stop Will from following the woman that headed into the bushes again. He could hear her terrible retching. "Damn it!"

Morning couldn't come anytime too soon. Ben didn't like having a sick woman on his hands. If anything happened to that child she carried, he would have to live with it the rest of his life. His heartbeat settled down when she finally came back and crawled under the blanket. "You want some water or something?"

"No, I'll be fine."

He wanted to argue with her, but she closed her eyes ending any conversation. He hoped she did go to sleep this time. Ben took a deep breath to quell his anger.

⚬⚭⚬

S ally groaned over the shove someone gave her shoulder to wake her up. Reality came too fast, and she didn't want to open her eyes and see the man standing over her.

"You'd best get moving, Mrs. Hooper."

Polite, she wondered why but was glad of it. She decided during the terrible night that this Ben must have come from the south. She couldn't help but wonder what drove him to be a bounty hunter. "He'd make his mama proud."

Sally rolled away and struggled to her feet. She didn't miss his reply.

"My mother's been dead a long time, Mrs. Hooper."

When she returned to camp there was a cup of coffee waiting beside her folded blanket. She felt her stomach roll, but managed to take a couple sips of the hot brew.

The sun was beginning to peek over the hills, she hoped the ride before her wouldn't be too long. When he moved, she stood up. "How far is this place?"

Sally didn't look away from his scrutiny.

"About an hour's ride."

She nodded, she handed him the blanket. "Thank you."

She didn't wait to see how he took her words, she couldn't care, but things could have been worse for her, and she owed him that.

The ride to meet Levi, filled Sally with dread. The man riding behind her tightened his hold over the weakness she couldn't keep back. "Will you let me talk to him, please?"

Ben's cheek rested against her hair, and he tried not to notice how good she felt. He didn't answer. He noted how heavy her accent became when she spoke of her husband. She'd asked him three times now and each time he refused to answer.

The mount slowed and Sally could hear the river. She said a prayer that no one would get hurt as they walked the horses closer to the river. There, by the crossing stood Levi.

The woman in his hold moan and his grip tightened. Ben could feel the tension racing through her as his gaze swept the area. He figured the Captain's men were here, but no one would do anything as long the woman was in the line of fire.

Anger vibrated through the man they rode up to. "Captain Hooper."

"Let her get down, Ben." Levi kept the other man in sight as well as Ben Frazier. "I brought her horse so she wouldn't have to walk to town."

"Your wife wants a word with you before we leave. Don't try anything foolish, Captain."

Levi nodded and walked up to help Sally down off the horse. He hated the way Ben's hands moved down her arms. Sally looked as if she was going to fall apart and he didn't hide his anger from the man.

His arms, oh yes, they were all she ever wanted to feel. "Levi..."

He pulled her into his arms. His hands moved over her as if he could right all the wrong or damage done. "Shh, I love you Sally. I want you to get on Beauty and ride to town, just follow the river honey and you will get there in no time at all." Levi felt her hands tighten on his shirt as if she could defy the separation.

"No! I'll come with you."

He looked into her pleading eyes and wished he could take away the pain he saw there. "Not this time Sally. The baby needs you to go home. Michael is waiting to take you home."

"My home is where you are, Levi."

Levi kissed her with all the longing and love inside of him. It nearly killed him to pull back, "Come on, I'll help you up on Beauty."

Levi turned with her and headed toward the horse. "I want you to follow the river, Sally, for me love, just ride away."

He couldn't look at the tears running down her cheeks. He put the reins in her hands and forced them to close over the rawhide. "Go on now."

When she didn't move the horse out Levi took his hat off and smacked the horse's rump. "Get out of here!"

He watched for a second to make sure she stayed on the racing horse. He knew one of the men would catch up to her.

"Come on Captain, we've a long way to go."

Levi took a deep breath before he turned to remount his horse. As he came up his hand slid under the horse blanket beneath the saddle, he heard Ben's gun click and stopped.

"Don't make me wound you, Captain."

The other man came around and reached under the blanket pulling out the gun, waving it like a trophy.

Levi schooled his face not to show any emotion.

"Mount up!" Ben's angry order filled the air.

Levi mounted without a word and moved in front of the man as his gun directed. "Are you going to point that thing at me all the way back to New Orleans?"

"If I have to, though I could just shoot you in the leg or arm or both, and be done with it. You wouldn't be as much trouble that way."

Levi smirked, "Might die, then you'd be out all that money."

"I may take the chance, now cross that river, Captain."

He tightened his thigh over the pistol beneath his leg, hoping it wouldn't slip. He chanced looking down the direction Sally rode, letting his breath out when he didn't see her.

"Ride Captain, your wife will be fine."

S ally pulled again on the hand covering her mouth until Jenkins finally moved it away. She hissed under her breath, "Damn it Jenkins, I couldn't breathe!"

"I'm sorry Mrs. Hooper, honest. Just couldn't let you make any noise—being so close and all."

She wanted to scream at him that she wasn't stupid, but there wasn't time. Sally walked over to his horse and pulled out the rifle.

She could tell he wanted to stop her, but the look she gave him froze him in place. Under her breath, "Where is Michael and the men?"

"They are all on the other side of the river. Michael isn't going to let them take Hooper."

"No, didn't think he would, but how about you and I get ready just in case they come back this way." As she talked she moved up to a boulder and found a place that gave her perfect aim at the other side of the river. She prayed she would not have a reason to fire the gun, but she knew she would if it meant saving Levi.

If she thought she could ride and shoot she would be doing that right now, but she was too weak to try. "Jenkins?"

"Yes ma'am?"

"If they come back I'll try to pick the one off toward the back, can you shoot the other one?"

"Damn straight."

She couldn't help but smile at the man's determination as he lay on his stomach with the other rifle. When this was over she had to remember to ask him why he had two rifles. For now, she brushed the thought off, and concentrated on the trail leading out of the boulders.

The shots in the distance made her bite her lip to stop her groan. "Stay safe Levi, I won't be worth living with if something happens to you."

The gunfire she heard made her eyes smart with unshed tears. She refused to be weak in any form as she stood there and waited, praying Levi would live through this.

The first rider broke free of the rocks, and then she saw Levi. By the way he was leaning in the saddle she knew he'd been shot. The third rider raced after them, and she couldn't tell which man it was and neither did she care. "Now Jenkins."

Sally took her shot and the last rider flew out of the saddle. Jenkins fired, but the first rider didn't fall, Sally aimed and fired at him. He fell.

"Watch them Jenkins if they move..."

"I'll shoot, don't worry."

Both of them raced out of the trees and towards the fallen men and Levi, now still and leaning over the saddle horn, it seemed as if time slowed down as Levi fell in slow motion to the ground. "NO!"

She heard a shot but never stopped running to Levi. Sally fell to her knees beside him and pulled him over onto his back. "Come on Levi, don't you even think about leaving us. We need you damn it!"

She held her breath as he struggled to open his eyes. She should be searching for his wound, but all she could do was smile into his gaze upon her. "Hi love."

"You're a hell of a shot, Mrs. Hooper."

Tears and laughter flowed out of her over his declaration. "Good thing too. Now, let's see what kind of damage you've up and done to yourself, Mr. Hooper."

Her gaze searched his body through her tears coming to rest at the dark spread of blood under his rib cage. "Damn it Levi!" She tore at her dress ripping off as much material as she could. Taking a deep breath she pressed the wad against the wound and held it. "Jenkins!"

"Yes?"

The man's answer came from right beside her. "I need you to help me see if the bullet went through."

He moved closer. Levi's hand gripped Sally's wrist above the cloth. "You did real good Sally, real good..."

His voice trailed off and she gasped. Jenkins' head lowered to his chest. "His heart is still beating, Mrs. Hooper."

Sally sucked in her cry, "Let's see if it is out of him. Real slow, we don't want to make it worse."

Together they gently rolled Levi onto his side so they could check his back. "Blood."

"It looks like it came through, Mrs. Hooper."

"Jenkins I can't tear my dress, please do it so we can get this bleeding slowed down."

The man got over his embarrassment and started tearing strips off her dress. "Make sure you get enough so we can bind it."

"Got it."

Together they wadded up enough material to put against the back wound. With Jenkins help they used the dress strips to wrap around his stomach to hold the bandages in place.

They were finishing up when Michael and the others rode up.

Michael was at her side before his horse stopped. She looked at him with the tears running down her cheeks. "The bullet went through, but he's...he's bleeding too much Michael."

Sally stayed strong for as long as she could, she couldn't stop the tears and Michael gathered her to him.

"Shh, Sally, he's strong, we need to get him to town and the doctor."

She came off his shoulder and nodded, knowing they needed to move fast. "I'm okay, thank you. Let's get him there. I think he would be better riding in front of you Michael."

"Yeah, better than the wagon." He tried to give her a quick smile as he squeezed her hand. "Can you ride, Sally?"

"Yes."

Jenkins left to get their horses and the men moved in to help get Levi on Michael's horse, she watched long enough to see Michael jump up and take hold of Levi and start out in an easy lope.

Sally rushed over to Beauty and with Jenkins help she mounted and took off after Michael with Jenkins and rest of them following her.

They rode into town at a fast walk, someone called out directions to the doctor office. Sally saw it was Mr. Billings, she saw him close his store and follow.

The sheriff met them at the doctor's. Sally ignored them all directing the men carrying Levi into the office. The doctor pushed them all out of the way to get to Levi, Sally refused to leave and the glare she returned to his own silenced any further order for her to leave. She stayed out of the man's way as he worked on her husband.

Sally moved up by his head and held his hand as the doctor worked.

"You did good putting that bandage on, stopped most the bleeding."

"The bullet is out, we think."

"Yup, went in from the back and passed right through, good thing."

She bit her lips to keep her question back, she didn't want to distract the man. When he started to stitch up the first torn hole, she looked at Levi's face. She kneeled down and whispered to him. "Darling, you are going to be fine. You're a strong man Levi Hooper."

Sally kept talking to him as the doctor worked.

"There, that's the last stitch."

She forced herself to look at the man. "How is he, doctor?"

"Like you told him, he's strong. He'll probably sleep a while, now we wait and hope he doesn't take on a fever."

Chapter 13
Time's Fine Line

"Sally, you need to come away for a while."

"No Michael, I'm not leaving him."

Michael looked at the doctor, and the man shook his head. Michael knew when the doctor sent for him that he'd had no luck getting through to Sally.

He moved over to her and squatted by her chair. Michael took hold of her hands to keep her from wiping Levi's brown. "Sally, look at me."

He waited, knowing she would, he smiled at her. "You look like hell Sally and you are so tired you can barely keep those beautiful eyes open. You need to lie down and rest, and get some food into you."

Her head shook, "I know, but what if he wakes and I'm not here? Hmm? He'd never understand why I wasn't here."

"Damn if he wouldn't, if he see's you like this he'll have all our heads." The stubborn set of her lips made Michael pulled out his last weapon. "You need to think of the baby, Sally. He needs nourishment, at least come to the hotel with me and have some dinner. Your trunk is up in the room and I'll order you a bath. I did that for Angie once."

"You did? Bet she loved that." Sally sighed, she knew he was trying to help her. "Alright Michael, but the doctor needs to promise to come and get me if—no, when Levi wakes."

She looked at the doctor and he nodded his agreement. "All right, I'll be right out, just let me tell Levi."

The doctor pulled Michael out of the room. "Give her a minute."

"How is he really, doc?" Michael stood stock still, it had been two days and still his friend hadn't come around.

"He's got a fever, not bad, but the next few hours could be bad if it rises."

At Sally's gasp the men turned and looked at her. "You didn't tell me that."

94

Before the doctor could answer she swayed and Michael reached her preventing her collapsed.

"She needs rest and food, damn it. You take her to the hotel, she probably won't wake up for a while. I knew this would happen, she's having a rough time carrying that child and if she doesn't get that rest there is no telling what might happen to her and the baby. Now get her out of here!"

Michael didn't argue with the man, he was beginning to fear for Sally as much as Levi. He looked down at her and the dark circles under her lashes. "You're exhausted and stubborn to boot."

Not that he could blame her, he knew she didn't want to leave Hooper, at least not until he woke. "Looks like it will be a race to see which of you sleeps the longest."

He called Jenkins over and asked him to bring some tea, crackers and cheese up to the room as he mounted the stairs. Michael kept walking right to the bed and with his foot bracing her up his free hand pulled the spread and sheet down.

Jenkins came in with the covered tray. "Just leave it over there for now. She'll need it when she wakes. Can you get her nightgown out of the trunk please and ask the manager to send up a couple of the maids and hot water."

Michael decided to sit with her in his arms until they arrived. "I'd undress you, Mrs. Hooper, but I'd probably get shot for the effort when he's better."

First Angie now Sally, he wondered when he would hold his own woman.

Once the maids arrived, Michael turned her over to them. They were glad to help, one girl brought washing cloths with her so they could clean her up. Poor Sally hadn't taken the time to change since this whole mess started.

Michael backed out and closed the door. He turned right into the waiting sheriff.

"Sheriff Gandy good see you."

"Guess so seeing as you haven't come down to see me."

"I am sorry, things have been crazy these last days."

"How are they doing?"

Michael looked back at the door. "Exhaustion final caught up with her and he hasn't woken up and is fighting a fever."

"We are all sorry about what happened. Those two were bounty hunters, you said?"

"Yes, I only know the name of the one that signed the note he gave to Mr. Billings."

"Your man brought it over. I telegraphed the judge you told me about and he confirmed that Mr. Hooper was cleared of all charges. I don't think you have to worry about any more of that kind showing up. The judge said that Mr. Black up and died, his widow called off the bounty on Mr. Hooper."

"Thank goodness."

"Who did shoot those two?"

Michael refused to tell this man that Sally did it. "I can't really say. We were all firing our guns to stop them."

"Who shot Mr. Hooper?"

"The other man, without the name."

"Doc said the bullet entered from the back and exited out the front."

The sheriff nodded over Michael's curse. "These bounty hunters have no morals. Well, I'll let you tend to the lady. I hope they both get through this."

"Thank you Sheriff." Michael stood there and took a deep breath. "All this for no reason, damn it all!"

⧉

Sally could feel the cold breeze brush her cheek and wondered why the mist didn't move. Everything looked distorted, and she raised her hand to see if she could push the foggy cloud away. When her hand seemed to go through the odd barrier she immediately pulled it back. Fear filled her entire being.

Her heartbeat drummed in her head against the suspicions filling her thoughts. She tried not to look at the scene beyond the mist, knowing it contained danger for her. No denial took the images away, nothing she did could stop them.

Aunt Bea stood by the window dabbing her eyes. *She's crying.*

Someone else was in the room, but she couldn't see him. It all looked stark and unfamiliar. Sally didn't recognize the place. Aunt Bea turned as the man spoke to her. Whatever he said made her cry harder. Sally wanted to go to her and comfort her, but the warnings and horrible feeling of danger held her back.

For a second she wondered why she should feel such fear, and she realized the answer stood before her. "The other side...of time. Oh, no!"

The admission sent a shiver racing through her, making her fight to breathe. Her head shook against time's pull—the fear overwhelming. "No! I don't want to leave him." She closed her eyes against the force, refusing to look any longer. Sally filled her mind with Levi, only Levi.

"No, I won't go back, I won't. Levi is here! Wake up, oh Sally, please wake up." She kept mumbling, repeating the command over her refusal to let it happen—to let time pull her back like it did—Angie!

<hr />

"Sally! Come on girl open your eyes and look at me! Please Sally, for Levi." Michael held her shoulders down to stop her thrashing. He couldn't say how long she'd been like this. He finally pushed through the door when she failed to answer his calls.

He couldn't help remembering what happened to Angie. Michael tried not to listen to Sally, knowing that her fear of going back—in time, drove the frightened words out.

Yes, this was the thing he knew she feared. Once his mind opened to the fact she came through time, Michael discovered many things about his friend's wife. The main one being she refused to mention time or listen to anyone that spoke of time, even the time of day. He witnessed the fear in her eyes no matter how hard she tried to disguise it.

His thumbs kept rubbing her shoulder. "Sally, Levi needs you. You can't go back there Sally. Your child needs you here just like Angie's child needed her. Come on Sally fight it and come back to us."

"Michael?"

The air sucked into his chest over hearing his name. "You are here Sally." He stared into her frightened gaze, "You won, Sally, you didn't go back."

She gasped and tried to smile past the teary sobs. Michael's grip on her arms finally eased back. "Thank you, Michael."

"You're a fighter Sally."

Sally swiped at the tears and returned his smile. "How is he, Michael?"

"Madder than a hornet."

For a second she closed her eyes and thanked God for letting Levi live.

Michael couldn't pull his gaze away, adding his own thank you for letting her stay. The fear still glared up at him. Michael could see her fighting for control.

"Won't the doctor let him up?"

"Nope. Levi doesn't like to be told no."

Her soft laughter brought the color back to her face. "He's a lucky man, Mrs. Hooper."

"Luck, could be it. Personally, I think it is magic."

He nodded and rose, "I'll let you get ready. He is also very impatient to see you."

"How long..?"

"He woke up yesterday. You slept for two days."

"Michael, please don't tell Levi about...about what just happened."

"I won't." He met her concerned gaze. "Do you think it is over?"

"I sure hope so."

Sally watched him close the door behind him. She pushed the covers off and sat up. The crackers on the nightstand made her smile. "You need to find your lady, Michael McFarlain."

Sally took a deep breath and tried to push away the worry over her brush with time. She refused to let it rule her life. "I am where I want to be and I'm staying right here."

⟨✤⟩

"Doctor Blance? Isn't there anything you can do?"

Roy wondered why the lady refused to let any other doctor touch this woman. She never liked him much.

"Well? You did get Angie to wake, do it for Sally, for heaven's sake!"

"Madam La Cross, I'm afraid your niece's friend is beyond our help. She suffered a major concussion that damaged her brain."

"How dare you give up!"

"I would love to accept your anger, but Miss Mercy is gone. We need to let her go."

"Get out!"

Belle glared at the man backing out of the door. Her attention swung back to Sally. "Sweet girl, please come back to me. You know Angie came back, I can't lose both of you, I just can't!"

The shell of the woman never flinched over her outburst. Belle's head fell to the bed as she wept for the girl that could no longer hear her. "I would even take your arguments, Sally."

When they called her to come to the hospital, she instinctively knew what to expect. "Joe Wind again...the man best stay at his mountain...."

It seemed he found Sally out on the trail frozen but still alive. Belle looked the girl over, "This isn't alive, no, she is back there with Angie." She brushed the blonde bangs back from Sally's forehead. "You went to find her and lost yourself, my dear girl."

Belle understood why Sally tried to find Angie, she regretted not staying close to her after the search party broke up. From all reports Sally ventured out into the mountain range to find Angie...alone. "Such a foolish move my dear girl. I won't find either of you, will I?"

She wished the girl could sit up and tell her off, but Belle already knew Sally couldn't hear her. "Just like Angie...gone from this life for another." Belle's lips brushed Sally's cheek. "Stay safe my dear and I hope you find your answer."

Chapter 14

Fate's game...

Sally brushed pass the curious onlookers in the hotel lobby. She didn't care what they thought of her, she probably looked a wreck. Levi was all that mattered.

Her search for Michael in the sea of faces lasted long enough for her to know he wasn't there.

When she stepped out onto the boardwalk her eyes automatically shut against the bright afternoon sun. She took a deep breath and forced her eyes open squinting to look out over the street. The congestion on the dirt street surprised her. For a second she gave into the pleasure of seeing all the buggies, buckboards and horseback riders on the street. She realized it wouldn't be long before the first cars rolled over these streets.

She made a mental note to speak to Levi about investing in certain areas.

Levi, the thought of him brought a smile to her. She stepped out into the bustle and dodged a buggy and some brave people trying to cross to the other side of the street. She was nearly running by the time she stepped up on the opposite boardwalk. She looked both directions and finally turned left in the hoped she would see the doctor's office. Her memory wasn't good and after going a few blocks she turned around and headed the other way.

Nothing she did seem to be working. "The Emporium, yes..."

Sally braved another rushed crossing of the street to reach Mr. Billow's store. By the time she entered the cool interior of the store she was out of breath.

"Mrs. Hooper!"

The man rushed to her side and guided her over to the chair she remembered well. Sally took deep breaths to fight off the rush of dizziness. "I am alright, Mr. Billows."

"I do disagree, you look too pale."

Sally force herself to smile and ease the man's concern. "I...it was the street, it certainly is busy."

"There are some trail herders in town."

"I see." Sally didn't but would figure it out later.

The words rushed out of her, "I can't find the doctor office and Levi?"

"Oh, I see, just wait a moment and I will close the store."

Before she could stop the man, he literally cleared the store of all his customers. No objection halted him.

Sally felt awful knowing she cost the man sales.

When he came back to her and took her hand placing it on his arm. "Let me escort you, Mrs. Hooper."

"I am sorry—your customers."

He smiled at her, "I only have one very special customer to worry over."

With that the man turned his sign to *Closed* on the door and escorted her out. Once outside he went to the right and headed down the boardwalk. Sally tried to pay attention but she was focused on seeing the doctor's sign. She did remember the sign from that dreadful day.

"Here we are, Mrs. Hooper."

Mister Billings opened the door for her and let her step in before him. The doctor came out of the room she knew Levi must be in.

"Mrs. Hooper, wonderful to see you. You do look better, rested no doubt."

"Yes Doctor, I did sleep."

"Exhaustion will do that to you." The man bowed slightly and waved her to the door. "He is not a patient man."

Sally smiled and nodded at the man, "I'm sure you are right."

She entered the room and couldn't dampen the smile or tears that flooded her face as she looked upon Levi. His attention was on the window and the activity outside. "I am here, Levi."

The way he swung about she knew it must have hurt, and she rushed to the bed. "Don't do that, my goodness you will tear your stitches and then we will never get home."

She adjusted his pillow and was reaching for the cloth to wipe his brow when his hand reached out to stop her.

"Sally, I'm fine, my love, just fine now that you are here."

She closed her eyes and breathed deep taking in the scent that Levi could fill her being with. "I know, Levi," her hand covered her stomach, "we know."

Ever so slowly she opened her eyes to take him in. All that was Levi stared back at her and Sally never felt happier. Her heart fill with the joy Levi Hooper always gave her. "Oh my only love, I am so glad to see you."

"And I you."

Sally caught the flare of anger in his eyes, "I slept."

"I heard."

"Michael?"

"He just left to find you."

She moved to sit on the bed beside him. Her hand reached out and cupped his whisker rough cheek. "You need a shave."

"Really?"

The humor in his voice finally reached his gaze, and she laughed softly. "Kiss me, my husband, before I go crazy!"

Levi didn't need a second invite as he pulled the woman of his love over his chest and kissed her with all the passion welled up inside. When at last he pulled his lips from hers he waited for her lovely eyes to open. His thumbs brushed away the trail of tears she no longer held back. "I missed you, Sally."

"Oh Levi, I was so worried..."

"I am fine." He smiled into her questioning look. "How is our baby?"

"Well, he is hungry, but I think the morning sickness has passed."

"Glad he smartened up."

"You know, we need a name for him."

"Only a boy's name?"

"Seems that is the way of things."

"I think you are right. I had some interesting dreams and a rather frightening one..."

Sally's hand gently covered his lips. "Let's look to the future, Mr. Hooper, only the future."

Levi waited for her to remove her hand. He didn't miss the touch of fear holding on in her gaze. "The future and our family, Sally."

She smiled, "Yes, our son, the ranch...and yes, we need to find a wife for Michael. He really needs someone to love."

Levi's laughter filled the room. "I couldn't agree more, Sally. He really needs a woman of his own. I never knew a man that could worry so much"

Sally couldn't help but laugh. She lowered her lips to his and kissed him as thoroughly as he kissed her. "We need to go home, Mr. Hooper."

"Anytime you are ready, Mrs. Hooper."

"How about tomorrow?"

"Sounds like a plan." He laughed over the look she gave him. "And no, I am not riding in the wagon."

"Oh, I don't know, it is the only way to travel."

Sally loved teasing him, and she wasn't above making her veiled threat come true. She needed to find Michael and get things ready. "We need to see what the doctor says."

"Did I hear my name?"

Sally sat up and turned on the bed to smile as the man came over to stand beside them. "Yes you did. Can Levi travel?"

"You two are not very patient people. If I had my way neither of you would move for a couple weeks."

Levi spoke up, "No sir, we have a ranch waiting to be run and a home to get ready."

The doctor shook his head but never lost his smile. The hope rose in Sally that they could be going home.

"I think you will be ready to go in two days." He held his hand up against the unspoken objections Sally could see Levi wanted to voice. "If the fever stays away another couple days, you should be ready to ride." The man looked at her. "Besides, your wife needs another day or two to rest up as well and I won't hear any arguments to the contrary."

Sally looked at Levi to see how he took the man's order.

"Alright, we will give it two more days."

"Good, then I am limiting your wife to a two hour visit then I want her to go get a good meal and go to bed. And you, also need to rest, Mr. Hooper."

Levi nodded to the man, his hand running up and down her arm captured all of Sally's attention. She wished they were alone.

The doctor finally left, but the visitors started arriving and Sally and Levi didn't have any time together.

By the time the doctor sent everyone out of the room and told her that her time was up, it was all Sally could do not to yawn.

"It was really nice that the men came to see you, Levi."

Her fingers absently brushed the hair away from his brow.

"I kept wishing they would leave so we could be alone."

His deep voiced felt like a warm breeze. She leaned down and rested her head against his chest. "We will have time together, Levi, I'm sure of it."

His fingers brushed through her hair, and she laid there loving the feel of his touch.

"I'm glad you are sure, Sally. Right now, I wish the waterfall was close enough for us to go to."

"Hmm, when we get home we will need to go there."

"Summer is almost over, soon it will be too cold to go."

She lifted her head up and stared at him. "Well, in that case let's take three days, the last one you stay with me at the hotel."

His brow rose in the most cockeyed arch, and she couldn't help but laugh.

"Sounds like a plan my dear wife."

"Oh yes, a real good one."

Sally delayed leaving Levi as long as she could. When the doctor finally forced her out of the room, she stepped out to a quieter town.

She stood on the boardwalk and took it all in. "My goodness."

"Yes, my thoughts exactly, it is too crowded in town. I will be glad to get home."

She accepted the arm Michael offered her. "Shall we go to dinner, Mrs. Hooper."

"I think I am actually hungry."

"I bet you are."

"Three days Michael, as long as the fever stays gone."

"I will get things ready for the trip home."

Sally smiled at her friend, "I can't wait to get home."

⚬✕✕⚬

Over the next couple days Sally spent every possible minute with Levi. She did take some time out for another stop into Mr. Billow's store. Blue material for the baby became a necessity when she realized they wouldn't be back to town for at least a year. Sally wondered if she would come to town the next time with a new baby.

When at last the doctor released Levi, Sally refused to leave his side. They had an early dinner with Michael at the hotel. The wink Levi gave her before they left Michael flooded her cheeks with heat and all she could do was stare back at the grin on her husband's face.

They wasted little time in reaching the hotel room.

She could see how tired Levi became during dinner, and she thought they might want to take it slow. "Levi...?"

"Come here Sally."

She moaned over the hold his arms took her in and his lips did little to smoother her desire for more. He pulled back and smiled down at her.

"I've been waiting too long to do that Sally."

"Me too."

His soft laughter tickled her ear as he buried his face against her cheek. "I don't think a night will cure me, my lovely wife."

Her cheek pressed against his as his lips explored her neck. "Hmm, how long will take to get home?"

He straightened to look at her, "Too long."

She smiled up at him and her finger traced the slight cleft in his chin. "Might be a good thing, but I would suggest that we sleep far away from everyone, my sexy husband."

"Shall we test how quiet we won't be?"

"Oh my yes, right now would be a good time to try..." Levi's lips capture her own. Her tongue ran over his teeth as his kiss deepened. She couldn't get enough of him. Sally worked at his shirt's buttons, she could feel his fingers brushing her hair to the side to undo her own. She wanted to be closer, touch him, feel him against her flesh, and she didn't care how it happened, she'd never been happier. That they nearly lost each other refused to leave her thoughts and Sally vowed that every single day would be special for them.

His lips moved over her shoulder and her head fell back giving him the freedom to explore. Her dress slipped off into a puddle at her feet, he made quick work of the undergarments.

Her frustration with the gun belt made her groan, and he stopped long enough to take it off and his pants. The touch of his warm flesh against her made her hug him tighter, and she wanted to drown in his heat. "Oh my love..."

Eager lips battled each other as her hands explored the man she came so far to find. Her fingers stilled over the bandage before her palm covered the area. When his kiss lifted she brought her hand up and buried her fingers in his thick hair. The brush of lips over her eyes gentled the breaths she fought to regain.

"It is alright Sally. Nothing will ever take you from me...nothing."

"Shh, my love, I know, I'm just grateful."

Levi kept his lips against her brow and Sally knew he too needed a moment to thank God for keeping them safe and together.

Slowly their lips and hands moved in gentle loving over each other. Sally felt the bed press into the back of her thighs, and she wondered when they moved to it. Her soft giggle floated over his shoulder as they both fell back into the giving mattress.

She looked up at Levi, "Love me Levi."

"Always, Sally, always."

His strong hands cupped her breasts as his thumbs explored the hardening nipples. She pressed up against his hard arousal, wanting him to drive it inside her with the force she saw in his eyes. Her hands gripped his arms as he took possession of her hips. They never broke the hold of their gazes as he readied her for his taking.

When she lifted her hips he met her with all the power in his possession and Sally arched to take him in. She felt complete with his manhood buried inside her heat. For a second they held the other there, within their hold as if affirming they were both real, both together, and both deeply in love.

Chapter 15
The Journey Home

"Levi! Levi, put me down, you are going to hurt yourself." Sally's laughter floated on the breeze.

"Never happen Sally, even with our baby growing inside you, you are still a wisp of a lady."

The cool water flooded over her sun warmed skin as Levi walked out into the blue pool of crystal clear water. Sally's laughter came as free as the waterfall now spraying the two of them.

"Are you happy, Sally?"

She took in the handsome man still holding her in the water. "Oh yes, Levi, happier than I ever thought possible."

"We made it home."

Her fingers played with the damp curls on his neck. "Yes we did and it was a fun trip without the cows."

His head went back in laughter. "What's the matter Sally, it couldn't be the lack of dust?"

Her nose crinkled up at his grin, "Hmm, I did like having you with me all the way home. Now, that my dear husband is much better than smelly, dusty cows." She looked around them, "And we made it back in time to enjoy our waterfall."

"Oh I am enjoying the view, my pretty lady."

Sally looked at her swollen belly sticking out of the water and laughed up at the wink he gave her.

"Now son, your mother is not laughing at you."

"I wouldn't."

"That's true, besides I think you are beautiful."

The loving way he looked at her caused a rush of heat to race through her. Levi slowly released her legs as he turned her to face him. Her lips met his in a gentle exploration. She pressed against him and slid her water slick body over his. Her leg came up between his thighs enjoying the texture of his warm flesh.

Before he could move, Sally wrapped her legs about his to bring her heat around his rod. She worked in a deliberate sensual rhythm over his rock hard erection. When Levi's hands lifted her up, Sally was ready to take him in. Her breath rushed out in satisfaction as he filled her being.

She didn't let him take her gently. Sally wanted to feel him rush into her, drive to the depth and touch the heart of her womb.

Their wanton cries joined the waterfall as they climaxed reaching a peak of fulfillment found together in love.

⊙∞⊙

"Mrs. Hooper, you aren't supposed to be doing that." Sally stopped in a mid stoop. "I just dropped the crochet hook, Marnie."

"So, call me and I will be glad to get it." The girl walked over and picked it up and in the same movement gently pushed Sally back in the chair.

Sally wanted to glare at the girl but forced herself to hold back. "It is hard to remember that I have you to help me."

"I am sure that once you get used to having me about things will fall into place."

With that the girl curtsied and left the sitting room. Sally stared at the empty doorway. She hissed under her breath. "Not likely, Mizzz Marnie."

She wondered again what exactly Levi had been thinking when he hired the girl. The doctor was the one to blame for the woman now a part of their home. *Your wife needs complete rest if she wants to carry the child full term.* Yes, she heard him tell Levi that news and her hopes Levi wouldn't react quickly faded.

The morning they were leaving to go home Levi met her at the hotel with Marnie in tow. Sally found out later that the girl had been one of the maids at the hotel.

Levi placed the woman up on the wagon with Bob. Their trip home wasn't to be a quick one as they both needed to take it slow. Sally was exhausted by the time they made it back to the ranch and Levi looked very tired to her. More than she liked she caught him rubbing at his scars. Once things settled down she coaxed Levi out for some alone time.

Sally's thoughts went back to their last trip to the falls, and she smiled.

Her hand automatically moved over her huge stomach. The weeks seemed to fly by once they were in their new home. Sally had to admit that Marnie was a huge help with the move into the big house. But she still found it hard to accept assistance from her. "A cook, maid and all round everything! So, what am I?"

The hands came from behind her and covered her eyes. "The prettiest mother to be in the Montana Territory?"

"Hmm, let me think, you must be some tall, sexy man that needs to be close to his wife?"

The kiss he planted on her lips was all the encouragement Sally needed. When he finally pulled back, she bemoaned the loss. "Now that takes away the sting from Miss Irish boss herself."

Levi laughed at Sally's curt remark. "Now Sally, she is here to help you. Didn't she get the curtains finished and hung up? And the pantry is full from all the canning the two of you did, more than you could have done alone."

She had to agree over the canning, they both knew she didn't have any knowledge of how to go about it. Without Marnie they never would have filled the pantry. "Don't rub it in, Levi. I just feel so darn useless right now."

He sat on the arm on the chair, his finger tipped her face up to look at him. "Hardly useless, you are very pregnant and Marnie is here to help. Accept her, my dear wife. You will have your hands full soon enough with our son."

"He should be coming soon, Levi."

He smiled down at her, "I figure within the next month."

She couldn't help but look towards the window and the first snow fall that started a little while ago. "From what the doctor said, he should be here before Christmas."

From the other room they heard the sudden yelling match taking place.

Sally smiled at the question in Levi's gaze. "Michael must have come in..."

"Ahh, yes, those two really haven't hit it off very well."

Sally's giggle filled the room. "Just a little conflict going on." She laughed once again over his raised brow. Levi's fingers teasingly pinched her nose.

"You are really awful, Mrs. Hooper."

"No I'm not, you and I both know..." her voice dropped to a whisper. "That they really love each other."

"Oh sure, like oil and water."

"You might be surprised, Mr. Hooper."

Levi didn't answer her right off, and she could see her words started him thinking, but before they could discuss it Michael came charging into the room.

"I never met a more stubborn woman! Why in the world did you hire her?"

Levi looked back at Sally and gave her a wink.

"She is fine Michael."

"Really? She is the most opinionated and bossy woman I have ever dealt with."

"Worse than Angie and Sally? Now that is saying a lot."

"No comparison!"

Sally rolled her eyes in a *I told you so look*. She watched Michael pacing in front of them and realized she'd never seen him this...animated. Oh yes, it seemed to her that Michael met his match in the Irish lass.

"Now Michael, she is a big help for me, she even taught me how to crochet." Sally held up the baby blanket she'd been working on. She wanted to jab Levi in his ribs for his snicker, but his bad side was beside her on the chair arm. "And she is an excellent cook."

Levi looked at Sally, and she could see he wondered what she was up to. He added, "She can cook, and those biscuits are yummy."

He smiled at the pouty look Sally gave him.

She wondered if she should be playing match-maker. It would be a difficult accomplishment. Michael seemed to take an instant dislike to Marnie. They'd clashed out on the trail the first day and hadn't stopped. Sally didn't think either of them would back down from their ongoing bickering.

Michael scowled at the two of them. "Fine, I'll give you that she can cook."

Sally smiled up at him. "Give it time Michael, she is still fitting in."

"We'll see..." He held up his hand before either of them could say anything. "She is here until the next cattle drive. I'll try to hold my temper."

The subject of Miss Marnie dropped as Levi and Michael walked off to the office discussing the feed stores for the winter. Sally watched the snow fall and wondered how bad the winter would be. She couldn't help but think of the spring flood that would come through the valley.

Everything was up on the plateau now. She pushed out of the chair and walked over to the large window. Her fingers gently touched the beautiful curtains pulled back to each side. "They did come out very well." Levi surprised her with a sewing machine once they unpacked the wagons. And he agreed that she could sew, but that Marnie would do all the hanging of the curtains.

Sally had to admit that the two of them did work well together. She liked Marnie and knew her only problem was her impatience with herself. "Pretty soon you need to come and meet this wonderful new world, my son. Besides, your mommy needs to be able to move once again."

She smoothed down the curtain's ruffle as her attention went out to the breathtaking view of the whole valley. She could see back a way and questioned how the horses were doing. Her own mare was in the barn and would foal this spring. She wondered what coloring the colt would have; it would be something if it were black with a white blanket.

The snow started this morning. Sally admitted that it looked beautiful the way it floated down and stuck to the trees. She couldn't imagine seeing it as deep as Levi figured it would get. She sure didn't want to be up in the mountains this winter, "Or any winter."

She smiled over the rolling movement of the baby. "Hmm, maybe it won't be long and you can watch the snow with me and your father."

Christmas seemed a ways off. Sally wanted to hold their baby. "We still haven't decided on your name yet. I'm leaning towards Ray or Connor, either are strong names. And you will need to be strong out here."

She could hear Levi and Michael talking about planting corn and hay next year for the livestock. Relying on nature wasn't going to last much longer with the growth of the cow and horse herds they were expecting. They needed to be prepared.

Michael ordered an extra wagon load of feed to be safe. The barn was filled to the brim with hay. Levi told her that they might need to feed the herds if the winter became too rough. Sally tried not to worry, but thoughts of the flood that would fill the valley told them all it could get very bad.

Sally let out a gasp over the pain that suddenly filled her back. Her hands rubbed at her lower back and she wondered if the baby would wait a few more weeks.

"Are you alright, Sally?"

She turned to face Levi as his hold came about her.

"Just some discomfort."

"I'll be glad when he gets here."

She nodded and smiled, "I'm right there with you on that, Levi."

His arm came about her shoulder as they both looked out over the increasing white valley. "The snow is early, Sally."

"I figured as much. You and Michael said we might not get a white Christmas. It is not even the end of October."

"Every once in a while it will snow early, but this one looks to be more than a couple inches. Michael figures that nearly a foot has fallen already."

"The wind looks like it is picking up."

"It could turn into a blizzard."

She looked up at the stern lines on her husband's face and figured she didn't want to know how bad a blizzard could be.

"I need to go down to the barn with Michael for a bit. Will you be alright?"

"I'm fine and Marnie is here. Could you ask her if she could bring in hot tea? And let her know I would like her to join me."

Levi's lips brush her temple and Sally wished it could be more. She couldn't help but smile over the thought. Sex wasn't something that could happen right now.

"I think I know that look, Mrs. Hooper."

"Really? Then by all means would you explain it to our son and tell him it is time."

"I'd say he is too comfortable to leave." He kissed her open mouth before leaving her. Levi's laughter followed him out of the room.

Chapter 16
Spring Thaw

Sally juggled the fussing baby up to her shoulder. Her hand gently rubbed his back. "It is fine Connor, your father is very careful."

Her pacing brought her to the bedroom window facing the valley once again. "Too much snow, now too much rain." Nothing but rain filled her gaze as she searched for any sign of Levi. "Why did he pick this morning to ride up the valley?"

She closed her eyes and took a deep breath, knowing that this morning had been the first in weeks without rain. When she looked again, she wanted to scream at the downpour now sweeping the valley. "Stay high Levi."

The baby let out a loud burp drawing her attention back to him. "Good one Connor, I hope you feel better." The boy cuddled up against her neck, and she sighed over the feathery touch of his warm breath moving over her skin. Sally realized the boy must be feeling her anxiety over Levi and Michael.

She checked the clock on the mantel confirming the late hour. They had left before dawn and it was nearly three. Though the days were lengthening, she knew it would be dark in a couple of hours. A sky full of clouds wouldn't help keep it light out for the two of them.

Connor's deep breathing told her the baby had finally fallen asleep. She walked over to his crib and gently laid him down. Her fingers brushed back the stray blonde curl on his soft brow. "Sleep little one."

Sally tucked the blanket in around him. Her mother's eye took in his length and figured he grew another couple inches. "You may be taller than your father if you keep this up."

It warmed her heart to know Connor was healthy and growing every day.

The rain started beating against the window and Sally's heart sunk. She straightened and walked back to check on the downpour. "It is getting worse."

She could barely make out the road leading up to house. Sally turned and rushed to the door making sure it stayed open so she could hear Connor if he woke. She made quick work of the stairs and rushed through the house to the kitchen. "Marnie?"

"I'm here, Sally."

Her friend stood by the window and from her movements Sally could tell she couldn't see any more than she did upstairs.

"How is the baby?"

"Sleeping, he finally settled down. I forgot how much of my mood he can pick up on."

"They do feel more than we realize."

Sally didn't ask Marnie how she knew that after learning that the girl came from a family of six, and she was the oldest. "I couldn't see anything upstairs, either."

"They will be fine."

The fist hold Marnie had on the curtain belied her calm words. Sally tried to lighten both their concern. "They are both careful men."

"But do they know the danger?"

Sally controlled herself from reacting to the girl's question. She didn't know about the flood. "I'm sure they will keep to the high ground."

"Yes, of course, they will."

Marnie walked away and started pulling things down from the shelves. Sally decided the girl needed to keep busy. "What are we making for dinner?"

"I'm heating a stew and I thought I would make a cake for later."

"What can I do to help?"

"The biscuits, you can do them if you like."

Sally gave the girl a smile. "I can do that now that I'm *taught well and good*."

She used the girl's favorite saying with Sally and earned a smile from her. Neither of them spoke much after that as they prepared dinner.

It wasn't long before Sally left to check on Connor. She refused to look outside at the darkening sky. Instead, she filled her mind with the planting that would need to be done. She and Marnie talked about the seeds Mr. Billings slipped in as a surprise for Sally. They would have a good variety on hand once they picked the best place for the new garden.

"It needs to stop raining some time."

The biscuits sat atop the stove staying warm. Sally was giving Conner a bit of the soup broth with smashed vegetables. His little arms and legs were moving all over with each spoon full.

"The boy likes his food, Sally."

She smiled up at Marnie, "Yes, he's doing good with it." Sally wondered how long it would be before he didn't need to nurse. She would miss that time with her son.

"I can see the lanterns lighting the road up the hill."

"Good, Jenkins figured it might help them. The rain must have let up some if you can see them, Marnie."

"A little..."

The sudden roar filling the house brought Sally slowly to her feet. She automatically shifted Connor to her shoulder. When Marnie turned to face her, Sally could see the fear in the girl's eyes.

"It's the flood..." Sally forced herself to walk over to the window. Her legs trembled so much she barely made it across the room. What she dreaded all this time finally came to be. She could see the rush of white caps coming down the valley. When it came to the house road she saw a couple lanterns disappear.

"Be safe my love." Sally turned and started racing through the house, she knew Marnie was right behind her. "We can see more from my room."

They rushed to the window in the bedroom and made it in time to see the wall of water reach the area where the ranch used to sit. It looked angry and mean, there were things, big objects rolling about in the wave of water. Over and over they would hear a huge crash and then the house would actually shake. She couldn't imagine what could cause it. Sally said a prayer that Levi and Michael weren't hurt.

No one said anything, the two of them stood there like sentinels and watched the angry waves of water flow through the valley. Sally wondered how long the wild river would keep running.

Eventually, they went back downstairs. Sally kept Connor with her and when he finally fell asleep she used the cradle he was almost too big for as his bed.

"Best make a pot of coffee, Marnie. I expect the men will be coming by on and off."

"Good, we won't sleep anyways."

Sally kept her hands from making fists, "No, I doubt we will."

"Do you think the water will come up this high?"

"I don't think it will."

She never thought the water could reach this far, but now that Marnie asked Sally started worrying.

The night dragged on and still no sign of Levi or Michael. Jenkins came by again and told her that the boys would be heading out at first light to look for them. He also told her that Levi and Michael most likely took to high ground further back in the valley where the flood started.

Sally tried to believe he was right.

Marnie never left her side and Sally was grateful for the company. Her friend was a strong woman, but Sally could see the strain of worry in her eyes.

Morning didn't bring much light with it. The rain still fell. The men left during one of the worse downpours. Sally figured that they needed to do something and nothing she said would delay their leave. She hoped they did find them.

Reverend told her that Jenkins and the boys were going to ride over the plateau. The higher ground would keep them from the flooded area and hopefully give them a better view of the water filled valley.

❧

Sally hated to look at the clock again, but needed to see how late it truly was, "two o'clock, the men have been gone too long."

She started talking to herself about noon time. The pots were still banging in the kitchen and from the loud knocks she figured Marnie wasn't in any better shape than herself. "Levi, so help me you must be okay."

Connor was playing on top of the quilt she spread out on the floor. Sally knew the baby looked so much like his father with her blonde hair. She wondered if he would be prematurely grey as well.

Sally's teeth bit at her bottom lip over her thoughts of Levi. After all they'd been through... "You will be alright."

The fists she held made her nails dig into her palm with her conviction. Without another word she walked over and picked up Conner. Sally wasted little time in reaching the kitchen. "Here Marnie, please take Connor."

"I would love to, but what are you planning, Sally? Your eyes say you are up to something."

"I'm going to go find Levi and Michael. I can't sit still and wait another minute in this house."

Sally saw the girl open her mouth then snap it shut.

"I'll be fine, I'm going to the barn and get Beauty. I have to go out to see if I can find them and the men. Something has to be wrong for the men not to return by now."

"Make sure you take your bedroll and I will fix you a sandwich."

Sally nodded, "Better fix a lot of them." She grabbed her coat and the leather poncho she wore on the cattle drive. "I'll come back once I get beauty saddled up."

"I'll have them ready."

Sally walked over and gave Connor a kiss on his brow. "Be good for Marnie."

Without another word she left them. Once out on the porch, she stopped long enough to realize the whole yard was a big puddle of water. She gathered up her skirt. "We could have a lake right here."

Taking a deep breath she moved out into the rain. The hard drops immediately pelted her as she ran for the barn. She slowed down once inside. The smell of hay hung in the air. She waved to the Reverend's hail and gathered up Beauty's tack.

The horse nickered to her bringing a rare smile to Sally. "So you are antsy too, Beauty. How about we go find our missing guys?"

"You think going out there alone is going to get them back?"

She turned to face the nervous man pacing behind her. "Reverend, we both know something is wrong or the men would be back by now." She returned to saddling the horse. "Besides, I've worn a hole in the carpet."

"I'm coming with you."

Sally wanted to argue but knew the man wouldn't listen. She tied a roll of rope on to the saddle and slid the rifle into its sheath. Sally stopped for a second, then reached into the tack room and took the gun belt off the peg and strapped it on.

She heard the Reverend walk up with his horse. "Marnie is making up sandwiches for the men, I'll go get them, while you saddle up."

He nodded and walked away.

She mounted Beauty and headed out of the barn and up to the house. Marnie was waiting on the porch with the bag.

"They are wrapped in leather, so the rain shouldn't ruin them." The girl passed them up to Sally. The bag's tie fit over the saddle horn.

"I'm sure they will be fine, Marnie. I know the men will love them." Sally tried to sound confident. "I will try to be back or send someone with news by nightfall."

"Stay safe Sally. Connor will be fine."

Sally forced a smile and turned back to join the Reverend now waiting by the road. Nothing more was said as the two of them headed up the plateau. Visibility was difficult in the downpour, but nothing stopped Sally from seeing the still raging flood waters ripping through the valley.

She forced herself to keep moving and concentrated on getting further back before it became too dark. More than once they came to places that showed evidence of landslides.

About an hour before dark Sally stopped to fire off two rounds of her rifle. She continued the signal every fifteen minutes until finally they received a reply and headed in that direction.

Sally thought they missed them and was ready to fire again when she saw Jenkins waving his hat. She dug her heals in and sent Beauty racing toward the man.

He took hold of the horse's bridle to still the animal. "Tell me, Jenkins."

"We found Michael, the boys are hauling him up the side now."

Sally looked over at the men and fought off her tears, "Is he...?"

"He's talking and cussing, so I think he is alright. Maybe a busted arm."

She nodded in relief, "And Levi?" Her question was barely audible.

Jenkins looked away a second before answering. "Michael said they both were caught in a landslide and he saw Levi being swept away. He managed to latch onto a root and was still hanging by it when we found him."

Sally sucked the air in her lungs that the man's words stole.

"I sent Richards and Waller out to search for Levi, they just came back before I heard your signal." He shook his head over her pleading look.

"No, he's out there!" Sally dismounted and raced over to the group of men that just got Michael up to the top. She knelt down beside him her gaze searching her friend for injury. "Oh Michael!" She tried to smile for his benefit. "I think your arm is broke."

"Yeah, sure feels that way."

Sally called out to Jenkins to get a travis started to get Michael home. "Make sure you get him to Marnie, and Jenkins please go in with him and take care of Connor so she can help him."

"You have been taking lessons from her, Sally."

She looked at Michael's half smile and realized he tried to ease her concern. "Yeah, well, you are in for it now."

His good hand came out and gripped hers. "He was still alive when the water got him, Sally."

She bent down and whispered to him, "I will find him, just take care of yourself Michael." Her lips brushed his brow.

He squeezed her hand before she pulled away. The men Jenkins sent out to search where standing by Beauty. The Reverend spoke up.

"They figured they could help so we don't waste any time."

"Good, plus the more eyes the better. He could be anywhere out there in that water, so really keep an eye out."

Sally refused to think about hypothermia or any other calamity that might affect Levi's survival. Reverend gave her a lift up onto Beauty. "Let's go find him."

They road as near the edge of land as they dare and every 15 minutes one of them shot off two rounds. She knew he wouldn't be any higher up than where they found Michael, but she did worry that he was on the other side of the floodwaters and with all the rain too far to see him. The roar of the floodwater could drown out the gun shots.

The only mystery Sally solved before sundown was the loud crashing and shaking of the ground. The water was so fierce that it picked up boulders and tossed them against the cliff at the flow bends. She refused to think about it and neither did she stop their search once the darkness fell.

The rain finally stopped long enough for them to make a fire and light torches, she prayed it would stay gone. The sandwiches were a welcome relief as they took to the saddles again. She made them ride in pairs with one of them walking the edge with a safety line tied to the walker.

She took the first walk too anxious to ride. More than once the ground beneath them would give way. Their signal shots came sooner in the darkness knowing that if he were out there now would be the time for him to hear them.

The search went slow, and for too many hours. No one questioned her order to keep going, even against their exhaustion. Sally, believed as the men, that the longer it took the less chance they had at finding Levi.

Chapter 17
Searching

"Levi!" Sally's throat was sore from yelling, but she refused to stop. Again, she fired her gun sure she heard something. She stood as close to the edge as she dare and called out for him. "Come on Levi, answer me damn it!"

The sun was starting to come out, and she wished it would hurry. She refused to move from this spot until she could really see to search the area.

The Reverend called out to her to back up. She did as he wanted knowing they didn't need anyone getting hurt. A couple more men joined them a few hours ago. They reported that Michael made it back to the ranch.

Marnie sent them out with more sandwiches and lanterns that did help in the search. They were being thorough with four teams searching. The Reverend already told her that once the land leveled out he would take the men with him, and she should head back up the valley and research the waters in the daylight.

Sally felt frantic over what the man didn't say. If Levi wasn't found above the ranch they would be looking for his body. She swiped at the tears that fell and were no longer hidden by the rain.

"No, I refuse to believe you are gone." She pulled the gun from the holster and fired another couple rounds. "Come on Levi answer me."

As if he heard her plea, she heard two distance shots. Her head swung about. "They came from further up!"

Reverend called out to the men to saddle up.

Sally mounted beauty and was heading back the way they came she made herself walk the horse not wanting to miss him. She pulled up and fired two more rounds and waited, "There, yes!"

She moved out again relieved that the shots sounded closer. This time when she pulled up she dismounted and walked to the edge to yell out. "Levi!"

Another two shots followed her call. Her frantic search found nothing. "Where are you?"

Reverend shot off another round. Levi's answering signal had Sally taking a cautious step to the edge, the shots were very close. "Levi!"

She caught the movement this time. Out in the middle by a group of rocks, she saw him. "There! He is there!"

His arm fell back to the boulder he clung to and Sally gulped her tears down.

"Reaching him isn't going to be easy."

"I know. He was too far out for us to see him before."

Sally wondered how they would reach Levi. "Reverend, send a man out to find a good thick limb. We can move upstream a bit and toss it out, the water will help take it to him."

The men felt her excitement and scrambled to get the ropes tied, while another went for the limb. "Reverend I think there is a smaller area just a little ways up that might help us get it out further in the middle. I can walk it down on Beauty."

Sally's patience was at its end by the time they reached the smaller area to toss out the tied limb. It took a couple throws to get it far enough out to flow out and away from the cliff. The rope was tied around her saddle horn, and she walked Beauty out, always watching the limb's progress before venturing much farther. She knew timing was everything.

Reverend let off a shot to Levi to let him know it was coming. She could see Levi trying to move around the rock. If he missed the limb, even if she stopped Beauty, it would rush past him, and they would need to try again.

Sally slowed it down a bit, but then feared it wouldn't be close enough for Levi. When he pushed off the rock, she let the horse go forward. Her heart was in her throat, and she nearly screamed when she saw him take hold of the limb. She stopped the horse and waited for Levi to get a good grip on the log.

She talked to the horse and started slowly backing her up. Her teeth bit into her lip over the fear holding her that he would lose his grip. None of them knew how hurt he might be. "Stay with me Levi."

When he finally vanished from her sight, Sally relied on the Reverend's signals to keep her backing up. Once his hand came up to stop she held the horse as still as possible.

The other men lowered ropes down to Levi. After a while she wanted to scream, not knowing what was happening. Reverend came walking over to her.

"You need to go over, he hasn't the strength left to tie off the rope. I'll hold Beauty, go on."

Sally nodded and dismounted, racing over to the men. One of them told her to lie down so she could get closer, but they needed to tie her off first. The rope cut into her ribs as she crawled to the edge to look over.

"Oh Levi." She gasped then swallowed her cry against how bad he looked. She could see a dark stain on his shirt telling her he must be injured. "Stay there Levi!"

At first, she didn't think he heard her and finally he looked up at her.

"Go back Sally!"

"No way Mr. Hooper." She moved herself over the edge and the boys started lowering her down. She didn't miss the curse coming from Levi and figured she would hear about it. "And I'll take it all, my love."

Once she entered the cold water she wondered how he ever managed to hold on as long as he did. Her arms went about his neck as he pulled her up against him. Neither of them said anything for a while. Sally finally pushed back a bit to look at him. "You look pretty bad Mr. Hooper."

He rolled his eyes at her. "You look marvelous, Mrs. Hooper."

Her fingers brushed away some of the debris on his cheek. "We need to get you out of this mess."

She took hold of the rope that needed to be tied around him. She worked it around him, under his arms and tied off the ends. "Hang on love."

Sally started to wave to the men to start pulling him up, but Levi took hold of her arm to stop her. "No, not until you are up, Sally."

She closed her lips to stop the argument she wanted to give him and instead jerked a couple of times on her rope. Sally held on as they lifted her, and she could see Levi's worried concentration on her progress. Once up to the top she leaned back over edge and waved to him. "Get him up here!"

The men worked quickly to get Levi up the cliff. Sally moved back and tried to stay out of the way, holding her breath the whole time.

She rushed to Levi once they pulled him up. He just laid there and coughed, she raced and got a blanket to put over him. His body was racked with shivers and new fears filled her.

The thought of the time lost in making another travis was dismissed by her. Levi needed more than they could give him out here. "Get him up on Richards' horse." She looked at the man and he nodded, knowing she wanted him to hold her husband. "We need to get him back as fast as possible."

Levi's teeth were chattering so bad he didn't say anything, but she knew he heard by the squeeze he gave her hand.

She rode beside them as they made their way back to the ranch. The men needed to carry Levi into the house. Sally had them take him to their room.

Marnie had water boiling and yelled at the men to carry the pots upstairs. The girl was a true wonder, Sally saw she laid clothes out for Levi and herself and also warmed the bed.

Jenkins came in and helped Sally get Levi out of his soaked clothes. Neither of them said anything as she dried Levi, and then they put him into the warm bed. Sally loaded the blankets on and tucked them in around him. Levi was asleep on his feet and he never woke.

Once things calmed down, Sally washed him with the hot water Marnie had the men bring up to the room. Sally took special care in cleaning the wound above his scar from the bullet. She stitched the deep cut and searched him for others, relieved not to find any. All they could do for him now was hope he didn't get sick. The tears rolled down Sally's cheeks as she thanked God for keeping him alive.

She refused to leave Levi.

Marnie brought Connor up to her and Sally fussed over the boy, both relieved that he could finally nurse.

Night fell and once Connor was asleep Sally crawled into bed with Levi and wrapped herself around him, hoping the heat from her body would help him.

She never released her hold around him. Sally finally allowed herself to give into the exhaustion pulling her down.

Chapter 18
Safe

Levi watched as Sally's delicate nose twitched. He moved a lock of her hair over her nose again and smiled. "You can't sleep forever my dear wife."

Her eyes slowly opened, and she smiled up at the man looking down at her. "I think I'm still tired, Levi."

"Me too, but don't tell Connor."

"He is probably hungry."

"He is just starting to wake up, we have a couple minutes."

Her hand reached up and rested on his brow. "No fever, thank goodness."

"That water was too cold for any heat."

She knew he tried to lighten her concern. "How did you ever last that long, Levi?"

"You."

Her brow arched, "Me?"

He nodded, "I kept thinking about the falls and how your slick body moved over me and the memory kept me warm."

She pushed him back into the pillow and moved over the top of him. "You are so bad."

Her soft laughter flowed around him and Levi loved the feel of her against him. "Want to warm me up?"

His fingers tangled in her hair as he met the force of her kiss with his own. Levi refused to tell her how close they came to never being together again. He'd lost his hold twice during the night and knew if they hadn't found him when they did he couldn't have hung on much longer.

When her lips suddenly stopped their decent done his stomach, he figured she saw the dark bruise over his ribs. "It will heal, love."

Sally studied him a moment to make sure he wasn't saying it to stop her worry. She moved her leg over his thigh and pushed herself up. "Glad to hear that." She gave him a smile. "It gives me the excuse to be on top." She moved in deliberate slowness over him. "And you know how I love the top."

Levi's deep throated laughter joined hers before silencing her with a heated kiss that soon had her beneath him once again.

"You feel so good, Sally."

Her hands framed his strong jaw. "No more floods, Levi."

His head turned and he kissed her palm. "I promise not to go out in one again, Mrs. Hooper."

Sally smiled up at him, "good, I can't take that rope again."

His lips gently roamed around the bruises across her stomach. When his exploration moved lower, Sally couldn't help arching to meet him. The feel of his heat against her own drove her crazy. The touch of his tongue over first one nipple then the other of her breasts made her moan break free for more. "Oh yes, suck me Levi, please, my love."

Her fingers buried themselves in his hair as he drew her in. Her hips rose under the music of his attention on her breasts. Her hand reached down and took hold his manhood, reveling in the feel of his need for her.

"Love me Levi, love me and don't ever let me go."

"My pleasure Sally and I swear we will always be together."

With his heated vow he plunged himself into her velvet folds. She closed her eyes over Levi's possession. They met each other thrust for thrust neither gentling the taking for they sought what they almost lost, and found the love that refused to be separated.

"I'm where I want to be with the man I love." Sally knew she found her answer.

The End

EPILOGUE

"Chase, come back here!"

"He's fine Sally, he needs to run it off. Trains are hard, too much confinement for the boys."

Levi was right, but she kept her youngest son in site as he ran about the depot. She heard Levi tell their oldest son Connor to go watch the boy and stay with him.

She took the hand Levi held out to her. "This is beautiful country, Sally."

The Canadian landscape was something to behold. She smiled up at the man so much a part of her life. "Thank you Levi."

His lips pressed into her brow, "No problem, Mrs. Hooper. It's been a pleasure."

He surprised her this year, after the herds were delivered, with the announcement that they would be taking a trip to Canada. Seems he heard of a tribe that settled north of the border. With the peace now in place with the tribes and the railway open he thought it would be a good time for them to investigate.

"I'm going to go see about transportation, the conductor said the road went up to the settlement."

"Alright, I will wait here and watch the boys." This train stop was the closest to the tribe's settlement they could find.

Sally smiled and waved back at Levi as he took off into town. The boys were chasing each other out in the field by the depot. Connor would be twelve this year and Chase six, they grew so fast it nearly stole her breath to think on it. Her hand covered her stomach, and she wondered if Levi decided on the trip because he knew she was expecting again. It seemed like six was their lucky number. "Will we find her, Levi?"

Angie had never been far from Sally's thoughts these last years. She always wondered how her friend was fairing and if she was happy. It was difficult not knowing, but she rarely spoke about Angie to Levi. She felt it best not to bring it up.

His announcement did surprise her. Of course the boys loved the idea of a trip on the train.

It wasn't long before Levi drove a wagon up to the depot. Once they were all loaded up and on their way, he told her what the livery said.

"He told me we would be there a little after mid day. Seems the settlement isn't too far away." Levi looked over at Sally and smiled. "And the man said that the tribe is very peaceful and that a woman speaks for them when needed."

Sally's breath caught in her throat. "A white woman?"

"He didn't say, only that she had the greenest eyes."

"It has to be her, Levi. You found her!"

"Calm down Sally. You know it might not be her."

"It is." She refused not to believe the woman was her friend.

His laughter rang out on the breeze and his hand covered his wife's now on his knee. "I suspect it is her. I sure hope it is."

Sally leaned over and gave his a kiss on his cheek. Their sons' giggling kept her from showing more affection.

"Hush now boys. When you have the love of a woman like your mother you will want these kisses and more."

Sally laughed at the faces the boys made over their father's words. One thing Levi never did was hide their love of each other from the boys. He said it would be good for them to know what love was all about so they could find it someday.

The further they went into the pines the more excited Sally became. Just the thought of finally seeing Angie held her on the edge of the seat.

Once the village was in sight, Sally was surprised by the number of people. She wondered how they would find Angie and Striker. Sally brushed the thought away when Levi up and asked the first man they came to where they could find Striker.

The man pointed and told him to go to the lake. Levi drove the buckboard deeper into the village until they saw the lake.

"I think we better walk from here."

The boys were out and already talking to a couple of boys that gathered about them. Connor asked if they could go off with them and Levi said yes. Sally ground her teeth down not to object.

Levi took her hand. "Let's go find your friend."

They both smiled to the curious looks and headed to the lake. Near the lake was a larger home made with more logs than Sally saw in the others. Her attention was immediately drawn to the couple at the lake. Their backs were turned she couldn't see their faces.

As they approached the couple, the tall man turned and Levi halted Sally.

"Striker." He nodded to the man that acknowledged him as well.

Sally's attention quickly went to the woman at his side. Her smile broadened. "Angie..."

"Sally!"

Levi let go of his wife's hand and both men watched their wives meet each other and immediately hug each other.

Striker moved to Levi's side. "She has waited a long time to see her friend."

"So has Sally, shall we let them talk."

"I see our sons have already met."

"Yes, right off." Levi looked at the man he always respected. "It is good to see their father as well."

Levi looked back at Sally and Angie, glad they finally found each other.

Don't miss out!

Visit the website below and you can sign up to receive emails whenever Jewel Adams publishes a new book. There's no charge and no obligation.

https://books2read.com/r/B-A-NXGC-LVOVB

BOOKS 2 READ

Connecting independent readers to independent writers.

Did you love *Answers In Time*? Then you should read *Gamble in Time*[1] by Jewel Adams!

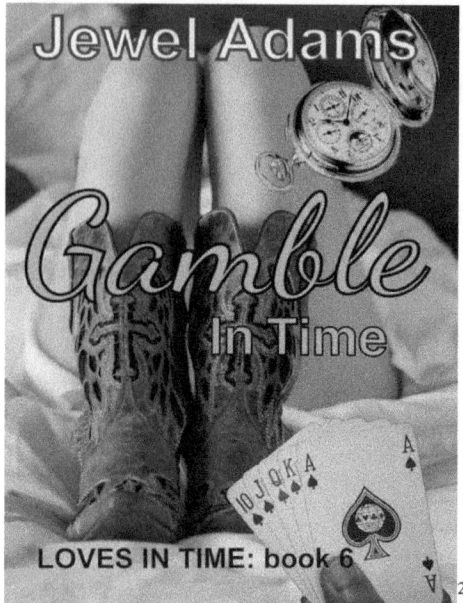

GAMBLE IN TIME

The renovated riverboat appears to be the perfect solution for her aunt's annual fundraiser. Angela La Cross's busy agenda didn't include falling into the boat's hold. When she comes to and finds she is the only woman on a boat full of men, she begins to think this wasn't such a good idea. James McFarlain wanted his last trip up the Mississippi to be uneventful. The last thing he expected to see on the Silver Queen was a woman. Telling himself she was nothing but a mess of trouble didn't stop him from looking into her emerald eyes. When she silently sought his help, James knew he was done for. Her trip back in time to 1875 became only a minor setback for Angie when compared to a good-looking cowboy, cattle rustlers, and one very determined Sioux warrior.

Angela might survive her tumble through time, but can her heart decide between the love of two men? Can she find the answers before time runs out?

---

1. https://books2read.com/u/menD6R

2. https://books2read.com/u/menD6R

Her journey is not an easy one when love keeps changing the rules. Join Angie in the adventure of a lifetime, one that will capture your heart!

Read more at https://authorjeweladams.godaddysites.com/.

About the Author

The last few years have certainly seen changes for Jewel. An outstanding author of over 15 novels and novellas, she will be the first to tell you that the Romance genre is thriving on the internet. As an author, Jewel found the freedom to take her love of Romance beyond the established barriers. Danger, love, tears, and romance; Jewel's Erotic and sensual romance Time Travels, Gothic, Paranormal, Fantasy, Westerns, and Contemporary Romances will take you on thrilling journeys sparked with adventure, and fill your life with the love that can cross centuries and worlds. Be sure to look for her new releases and news at the following sites:

https://authorjeweladams.godaddysites.com/ https://author-jeweladams-lilysimmons.com/ http://www.facebook.com/jeweladams http://twitter.com/JewelAdams Email her at: jeweladams@gmail.com

Read more at https://authorjeweladams.godaddysites.com/.